THE
SCARLET
CANARY

•

Jack Lewis

AVALON BOOKS
NEW YORK

PRINTED IN THE UNITED STATES OF AMERICA
ON ACID-FREE PAPER
BY HADDON CRAFTSMEN, BLOOMSBURG, PENNSYLVANIA

This one is for Brandon,
who has traveled the hardest road of all!

Chapter One

The kid was worried, and I could understand why. I'd done my share of cheap pictures when I was getting started in Hollywood. Some of those Poverty Row sharks who call themselves producers don't care whether you live or die, as long as the stunt looks good on film.

Long before my time, a producer went down to L.A.'s skid row and hired a drunk to go up six stories and swing hand-over-hand on a stretched rope to a building on the opposite side of the busy street. The poor lush didn't make it, and after bouncing off the top of a Ford convertible he ended up dead in the street. When the film was released, the producer had the poor taste to advertise with the statement: "Never Before Filmed—The Actual Death Of A Movie Daredevil!" Even with that kind of promo, it didn't get many play dates, proving that most theater owners have better taste than their suppliers. Some good did come out of that and similar shockers, though. The fall guys got together and formed the Motion Picture Stuntmen's Association as a means of bringing professionalism to the business, and guarding against abuse by producers.

"What do you know about this outfit?" Georgie Huerta asked, plainly worried. I shook my head. From what he had told me thus far, it sounded like one of those hit-and-run outfits that turn out films cheaply, then send them directly to video because they know they're never going to get a deal for theater release.

"Nothing," I told him. "Never heard of the outfit. Give me the whole thing one more time, but slowly."

Staring into his coffee cup, Georgie explained that he'd gotten a call to do the stuntwork on a little Western being made by an independent producer. Actually, it was a cross between a cowboy show and a horror flick, but that wasn't important. What was important was one of the stunts, which called for Georgie to ride hard to catch the heroine, who ducks low over her horse's neck as she jumps a log and rides on. The stuntman, doubling for an actor portraying a bad guy, is riding behind her. His horse jumps the same log, but he doesn't duck. Instead, he is swept off his horse by an overhanging branch.

"That's enough," I told him, holding up a hand. "That gag'll get you killed, unless it's rigged right." Hollywood pros refer to their stunts as "gags."

He offered a sullen nod. "That's what I've been tellin' 'em, Charlie, but they ain't hearin' me. They're talkin' about gettin' some other guy who won't worry about it."

"Anyone who'll do that gag the way they want it is not a stuntman. He's a mindless fool, Georgie." I guess my tone was more a snarl than an observation, because the man sitting across from me in the booth slid back on his seat, showing surprise.

"Who's the stunt coordinator on this?" I asked. Huerta shook his head.

"They ain't got one as far as I know."

"Then who's the director?"

"Fellah named Peter Langley."

"Oh! *Him?*" I couldn't keep the disgust out of my voice. Peter Langley had been a script clerk on other low-budget films being shot for release only on video cassettes. No telling how he'd gotten to be a director.

"Got a phone number on him?" I asked, taking a business card out of my pocket and reaching across the table to slip a pen out of Huerta's shirt pocket. Like me, he wore Levis, worn cowboy boots and a Western-styled shirt with snaps instead of buttons. The last time I saw him, he was a kid. Now he was in his early twenties trying to make it as a movie stuntman. I was almost twice his age and trying to get out of the business. Considering my standing—or lack of it— back on the Mescalero Apache Reservation I'd once called home, I was surprised he had come to me for help.

He reeled off the number and I wrote it on the back of the card, then slipped out of the booth. He started to follow me, but I shook my head. "You stay here. I'll be back." I turned and went to a side door to the coffee shop. It led into the lobby of the hotel where I lived, which is where the phones were.

I dialed and a man's voice answered, "Reel World Productions."

"Is this Peter Langley?" I demanded. There was a moment of silence before he admitted it was.

"That must be some outfit, if the director's answering the telephone," I observed. "This is Charlie Cougar."

"Good to hear from you, Charlie," he ventured carefully. "If you're looking for work, we've got everything covered."

"You do not have everything covered, you idiot. You're going to get a stuntman killed!"

"George Huerta, you mean?" His voice was suddenly neutral, choosing each word with care. "What does he have to do with you, man?"

"He's a Mescalero Apache. One of my tribesmen. I'm looking out for him."

"What's the problem?" Langley wanted to know, suddenly defensive. "What's he been saying?"

"He hasn't been saying much. I'm the one doing the talking," I told him. "That gag with the tree limb is for fools and amateurs, the way you're planning it!"

"We'll get someone else to do it, if he's afraid," Langley stated, his tone turning cold.

"No, you won't get someone else. You'll do it right. You need a tree limb made out of balsa wood, hung on that tree from a hinge. That way, when his horse jumps the log, Huerta can throw up his arm and the balsa wood won't hit him in the face. And when the limb swings back on the hinge, it softens the force of the contact."

"That sounds like a lot of money, Charlie. We don't have the budget to rig that kind of stunt." He was back to being cautious again.

"You'd better find it, then. Columbia used a limb like that in an old Randy Scott picture years ago. Jock Mahoney did the gag. That limb's probably still in their prop shed, if the termites haven't gotten to it. You rent it and I'll help the kid rig the stunt."

"I don't know," Langley hedged. "Maybe we'd better look around for someone who's hungry."

"Maybe I'd better call the Actors Guild, the Extras Guild, and the Stuntmen's Association and tell them what you're up to, and that you're going to get a stunt-man killed. Whoever's putting up the money for this two-dollar epic ought to love that kind of publicity!"

I could hear the sigh of defeat after a moment's consideration. "Okay, Charlie. I'll call Columbia."

"And get someone to help him rig it!"

Back in the restaurant, I found Sam Light sitting across from Georgie, playing with a cup of coffee.

"I think I've found you a job," Light said, as I slid in across from him. "Something semi-respectable. You're going to work for Jonathon Doom." There was something about his smile I would have considered downright evil, had I not been so surprised.

"That flake? What can I do for him?"

"He's a *wealthy* flake, Charlie, and you won't have to fall off horses to pay the rent," Light offered. I switched my attention to Georgie Huerta.

"I talked to Pete Langley. He'll get the balsa limb

and someone to help rig the gag so you don't kill yourself. It'll be a piece of cake." Georgie nodded and smiled as I turned my attention back to Sam Light.

"I'd better get outta here," Georgie murmured. "Got things t'do. Thanks, Charlie." He was smart enough to know that what was coming down now was none of his business. I nodded at him as he slid out of the booth.

"Call Peter and stay in touch on that tree limb," I told him. "I don't want him to weasel his way out of this."

"Like cockleburrs in a steer's tail," Georgie promised, grinning and offering me a wink.

I sighed. It would be nice to be that young again. I turned my attention back to Sam Light. "Okay, tell me about Lenny Squiglemayr and what madness he's planning now."

Chapter Two

I don't know who you are, and you probably don't know me either, but if you paid good money to read this book, I reckon you deserve to know a little of my background.

My name is Charlie Cougar to most people. It's a show biz name I picked up when I started riding in rodeos. My legal name is Charlton DeMille Smith, and that's a monicker no Apache would want blasted over a rodeo sound system. It all came about because my mother saw Charlton Heston playing Moses in a Cecil B. DeMille movie when she was carrying me. So much for that.

I'd come back to the Mescalero Apache reservation in New Mexico when I was 19 after a fairly successful rodeo season. Some of my rodeo friends showed up and we started drinking—that's when we decided to round up some of the tribal horses and sell them. When it was all over, I was the one facing the music, and I was banned from the reservation for life. The Federal Bureau of Investigation gets involved in a lot of reservation problems, because a reservation is classified as federal land. I probably could have gone to prison, but someone decided to let the tribal elders handle my case. Being banned from my home and family was worse to me, I thought, than going to jail. When you lose your roots, I'd always been taught, there's not much left.

I went back on the rodeo circuit and finally sobered up with the help of some riders who belonged to Alcoholics Anonymous. Then I found I could make money every time I fell on my head, instead of just the times I won a rodeo event—working as a stuntman in Hollywood. With the help of other one-time rodeo stars who'd settled in Hollywood, I learned the ropes and made an on-again, off-again living by doing gags that required little common sense and an intense instinct for survival.

I'd learned to do other things, too, in order to eat regular meals. Having a backup occupation of some sort is a requirement to work in the film business, unless you're at the top level. If you don't believe me, check the used car lots in the L.A. area and count how many familiar screen and TV faces you see working as hucksters.

I met Sam Light at an Alcoholics Anonymous meeting and we'd hit it off right away. Both of us tend to be loners, I guess, and there was an instant mutual respect for each other's space and privacy. Sam was not one to talk about himself, but I learned he had been in the Marines for a couple of hitches before he got serious about newspapering. Now he was head of the Los Angeles bureau for a San Francisco news syndicate. Sometimes I worked as a leg man for him, checking out facts or running down individuals. As a one-time process server, I knew how to find people— even those that didn't want to be found. That was an asset in working for Sam.

Several months back, the two of us had been involved in solving the murder of a retired stripper, and finding the treasure her racketeer brother had left behind. That got Sam Light promoted, but it hadn't done much for my film career in spite of the publicity.

The average working life of a movie stuntman is about five years. By that time, he is usually so tired and beat-up that he becomes a danger to himself and sometimes to those around him. The smart ones retire and buy bars or bowling alleys. The not-so-smart ones all too often end up in a graveyard or as bedded vegetables at the Motion Picture Country Home and Hospital in Woodland Hills.

As a semi-senior stuntman, I had gotten a few jobs as a stunt coordinator, mostly on televison shows. That's the guy who tells other stuntmen how to keep from getting killed, yet still manages to get what the director wants on film. A few even go on to become second unit directors, handling the action stuff on locations far from the studio. I had no delusions that I'd ever end up in that league. I'm just not a people person. And that's not just my opinion, understand. A lot of people have said it, even some of my friends!

A lot of stuntmen entered the trade as I had, coming from another field of physical work. Today, though, the town is full of would-be fall guys who've just graduated from stunt schools. These institutions of higher learning are not like a lot of others. There's an old saying that "those who can't succeed, teach," but most of these schools are run by older, experienced stuntmen past any residual desires to risk their own necks. The majority of these new graduates are so clumsy they can't get out of their own way! Still, they are young, ambitious and willing to learn. That thought caused me to reflect from time to time that my days were numbered, if I didn't want to end up as one of those vegetables. That was among the reasons I had let Sam Light and a few others know I was seeking other routes of honest endeavor.

Another reason was a Lakota Sioux lady named Sue Tallfeather. She was sort of my girl, or so I thought. We spent a lot of time together, but she was bent on getting a degree in computer science, and she didn't always approve of my reservation-born simplification of life and its trials.

I had been filling the spots between movie jobs by working as a process server, until I chased a guy across a pet cemetery. I'd stumbled over a dog's tombstone, and the servee got away. When I was able to sit up, I was nursing a broken ankle and looking at a small tombstone inscribed:

We Love You,
CHARLIE
Rest in Peace

About then I figured Somebody Up There was trying to tell me something. And the ankle had put my stunting career on hold for two months, causing me to miss a couple of good jobs. I finally had to agree with Sweet Sioux—I called Sue Tallfeather that from time to time just to watch her burn—that there is no future in chasing people through cemeteries or anywhere else!

Now I was sitting across the table from Sam Light, who just told me he had arranged for me to work for a guy I'd known as Lenny Squiglemayr. That had been his name until he had it changed legally to Jonathon Doom, a character he had played for several seasons in a top-rated television series. But that show had been put on ice five years ago, and eventually even the residuals from reruns disappear.

"What's Lenny up to now?" I asked my friend.

"Jonathon Doom," Light corrected, keeping a straight face. "Maybe he'll let you call him Jon when you've worked for him awhile."

"What's Doom up to now?" I asked again, picking my words carefully.

"He's incorporated a company he calls Trouble, Incorporated."

"How can he do that?" I demanded. "That was the name of the outfit he ran in the TV shows! In fact, it was the name of the series!"

"He created the show, remember?"

I didn't remember. I'd worked on a few of the shows, even doubling for the star a few times in fight scenes, and had once had fallen a horse for the actor who'd portrayed the heavy. I'd considered Doom just another actor who'd caught a plum role and had ridden it to the end.

"By creating Trouble, Incorporated, he was protecting the characters and the other components when he copyrighted the material. Now it all belongs to him," Light explained patiently.

I offered a shrug. "Maybe he's smarter than I thought he was."

Light nodded. "Obviously, he's smarter than a lot of folks thought he was."

"But where do I fit in?"

"You're going to have to take that up with Doom. I gather you'll be doing much the same thing you've done for me. You'll find people for him, do research on certain subjects, and maybe even serve as a bodyguard on occasion."

I thought about it for a few seconds, running the possibilities through my head. In the TV show, he'd had an assistant, who wasn't too bright. From my observations, the script writers didn't have to work too hard to make that particular actor look stupid. It was classic type casting. I wondered how stupid I was supposed to be as Lenny's stooge.

"How is this thing going to pay?" I wanted to know. "What kind of future does it have?"

"You'll have to work that out with Doom, but he told me you'll consider the pay ample." He offered me a pitying look. "Handle it right, maybe he'll make you Jonathon Doom, Junior!"

"That'll be the day." It had been more than five years since I'd seen Lenny—I mean, Jonathon—and I was trying to remember whether I'd liked working with him.

I liked the premise of the show and the way it was set up. Doom, if he was the creator, had stolen a gimmick from an old Robert Montgomery film, *Lady in the Lake*. In that movie, the only time one saw Montgomery was in a mirror, or maybe as a reflection in a pool of water. The entire film was shot from the camera's perspective. Jonathon Doom had followed the same, formula, using his voice to narrate, which saved a lot of dialogue with other actors. It also saved a batch of production money. That, of course, made his sponsors happy, and there seemed to be millions of people who'd never seen the old Montgomery film. Everyone thought Doom's approach was neat and original.

Sitting there, thinking about it, I accepted the fact that Doom hadn't left much of an impression on me. I did recall that I had been involved in a fight scene, and kept pushing punches at the camera while I grimaced at fists that were hurled at me by another stuntman. It had gone down in my book as a strange but rather lucrative experience.

"When am I supposed to get together with Doom?" I asked Light. He shrugged and handed me the business card he'd been turning end over end throughout our conversation.

"Give him a call and set something up." He was sliding out of the booth, grinning.

"You got anything for me to do meantime?" I asked. He shook his head.

"I may have to put you on the night shift, if Doom's

going to work you days." He raised a hand in salute. "Go see what he says. I have to get out of here."

I downed a cup of cold coffee while I thought about the work I'd been doing for Light, what it would be like to work with Jonathon Doom, and the promise I'd made young Georgie Huerta. The future suddenly seemed very complicated.

I went back to the hotel lobby and called the number on Doom's business card. I recognized his voice when he answered.

"This is Charlie Cougar," I announced somewhat cautiously. "A gent named Sam Light said I should call you."

"Ah, yes, Mr. Cougar," the heavy baritone voice responded. "I remember you from the series. You're the Apache Indian."

"Yes, I am."

"I had a long discussion with Mr. Light. He's doing a feature story on my new enterprise, and he felt you might be able to fill my needs. When can we meet?"

"I'm free all afternoon," I told him. "How about now? Where do you live?"

He gave me a Beverly Hills address. "I can be there in less than an hour," I told him.

"I look forward to it," he promised rather grandly, and hung up.

In terms of social and economic status, there are light years of difference between where I live in Gower Gulch and the Beverly Hills city limits, but on a map of the Los Angeles street system, it's only a few miles. I hadn't shaved that morning, so there was time for that, I figured.

The hotel I have called home since arriving in Hollywood has two advantages: it's close to several of the studios and, more importantly, it's cheap. The six-story structure was built in the early 1930s, when Hollywood was the Golden Dream for a lot of people. Now it was a senior citizen among the other lodgings, and was known along the boulevard as Heartbreak Hotel. It was home to a lot of movie technicians, a few of them retired; to a few minor actors and wanna-be actors; and to a lot of male victims of divorce.

I tried not to tell people where I lived. If I even mentioned the area, a lot of people looked down their noses. But it was the first place I'd found when I landed in Hollywood, and I'd become comfortable there. I knew all the personnel in the hotel, the adjoining bar and the coffee shop. Because of my length of tenure, I had perks that no one else got. For example, behind the hotel was a parking space with my name on it. The only other person with that kind of clout was the hotel manager.

Sue Tallfeather knew where I lived, but she'd never been in the place. She'd picked me up near the bus stop in front of the hotel several times, but I had the good sense never to invite her past the front door. Down deep, I feared she'd turn up her nose at the place, as some others had done, but she'd never commented on it. Those of us who lived there tended to refer to the structure as "architectural antique." Others in the neighborhood regarded it as a firetrap.

I took the elevator to my floor and went about shaving my almost nonexistent beard. Then I took a quick shower. I wore an old flannel shirt and faded Levis for my coffee shop meeting with Georgie Huerta, but that didn't seem appropriate for Beverly Hills. When I left the building and circled the structure to the parking lot, I looked like a dude on his way to a rodeo. I had on a Western-cut suit, polished Tony Lama boots, a cowboy shirt and a matching turquoise-inlaid buckle and bolo tie. On my head was a ten-gallon cowboy hat I'd never worn before, with a Sioux-beaded band and an eagle feather.

I might have looked better in Beverly Hills in a custom-made business suit, but I didn't own one. Nor did I want one. As a lone Indian in Hollywood, I rather enjoyed the identity.

My ten-year-old Ford truck was sure to raise eyebrows in Beverly Hills, too, but it's difficult to haul a horse trailer and saddles behind a Ferrari or a Lincoln. Besides, the truck was a status symbol in itself. I'd had several other stuntmen try to buy it from me. I knew what they really wanted was the six-foot spread of Texas longhorns I had attached to the hood!

Chapter Three

I had to pull up to the curb and look at my map once I'd passed the sign on Sunset Boulevard that marked the Beverly Hills city limits. I found the street on which Jonathon Doom was located and headed for it, the map book on the seat beside me. I hadn't gone three blocks before I noticed a black-and-white tailing me. It was lying back perhaps a hundred yards, but each time I made a turn, the police unit followed. I could see that a second officer was seated next to the driver. Maybe Beverly Hills was more dangerous than they advertised!

The street turned out to be a residential area made up of condominiums and apartment buildings. I spotted Doom's building and circled to an alley, scoping out a parking space. I finally found one and pulled into a stall marked *Visitors Only*, the police car wheeling in beside me. I pretended to ignore the two men in the front seat as I got out of the truck and carefully locked the doors. They got out, too, and came toward me, smiling and friendly, but one of them had his hand near his holster. You never know these days, I figured. Not even in Beverly Hills.

"How you doin', Tex?" one of them asked. I shook my head. He wore a name tag that identified him as Smith. The other man's tag said Jones. Whoever made up their duty roster had to have a sense of humor. A long-ago television series, *Alias Smith & Jones*, had been about two Old West outlaws trying to go straight without a great deal of success.

"I'm from New Mexico," I told them.

"We thought you had to be from Texas, wearing a hat like that," the other man ventured. He was inspecting the rack of horns on my hood as though he suspected I'd rustled the steer they came from. "You a cowboy?"

"No." I was playing it cool. "I'm Native American. Mescalero Apache."

"What's the reason for that feather in your hat?" Jones asked, frowning.

"It means I'm an Indian," I announced evenly. "I'm allowed to wear it."

"Allowed? What's that mean?"

"It means I'm an Indian and I'm allowed," I repeated slowly. "By act of Congress, the only people in the United States allowed to possess eagle feathers or eagle claws are Native Americans and Boy Scouts. If anyone else has feathers or claws in their possession, it's a Federal offense. A felony, I believe."

Jones shook his head doubtfully. "I was a Boy Scout. I never got any eagle feathers, though."

"Should've taken it up with your Scout Master," I told him. I was beginning to enjoy this exchange, but I didn't want to be late for Jonathon Doom.

"You got a driver's license?" Smith wanted to know. Without answering I slipped my wallet out of my back pocket and unfolded it to show him the license. He told me to take it out.

"Charlton DeMille Smith? That's your name?" He didn't seem particularly pleased that we both had the same last name.

"I work in pictures as Charlie Cougar." I knew that what was taking place was more or less standard procedure for Beverly Hills. The city has a great reputation for guarding its citizens from irritating outside influences like door-to-door salesmen, vagrants, panhandlers, the homeless, and probably wandering American Indians as well.

"You're an actor?" Jones was looking me up and down carefully, as he returned my license.

"A stuntman." I nodded toward the building behind them. "I have an appointment in there with Mr. Jonathon Doom."

Mention of the name caused the officers to look at each other, amusement showing in their eyes. They must have remembered the old TV series.

"Okay," Smith said, tone either friendly or condescending. I figured the latter. "No problem. You understand why we stopped you—we don't see many steer horns here in Beverly Hills. Have a nice day."

"You, too," I said, as I slid the license back in my

wallet. They were driving away as I crossed the parking area and trekked around to the front. I found Jonathon Doom listed as a tenant.

The man I knew as Lenny Squiglemayr opened the door to his condo. He hadn't changed a great deal in the years since I had seen him. He stood about six feet two, with a pair of broad shoulders that seemed to have narrowed just a trifle since we'd worked together. He wore a pair of designer jeans, a polo shirt, and sandals without socks. It only took me a moment to note that his toenails were carefully trimmed and looked as though they were coated with clear nail polish. His hair appeared to be his own, although it was graying about the temples. He had the same thin-line mustache he had worn in his TV series. I always felt Squiglemayr—now Doom—looked too much like the late actor Jack Cassidy to make it far in films. Television, though, invariably seems to settle for less.

"Glad you made it, Charlie," he declared, clapping me on the shoulder like an old friend and dragging me into the room. "We've been waiting for you!"

I had been so surprised by the greeting that I hadn't noticed the elderly man seated near the window, looking out to the street below. He rose as Doom led me across the room to face him. I managed to take off my hat on the way.

"Mr. Teller, this is my assistant, Charlie Cougar. He's a genuine Apache Indian!"

Teller was looking me up and down with a frown, probably wondering whether this was some sort of joke. Or perhaps he was wondering how one would go about identifying a non-genuine Apache. Finally, he extended his hand, and we exchanged testing grips, firm but without too much pressure. "Glad to meet you," he said. "I'm Simon Teller."

I knew the name. I'd seen it often enough in the business section and the society pages of the Los Angeles and Beverly Hills newspapers. I gathered he stood on a pretty high rung of the Southern California social ladder. As far as I knew, he was an astute businessman and was respected both for his business acumen and his conduct in his personal life.

"Let's all sit down," Doom suggested, pointing to chairs. I noted that he had poured a drink for Teller. It was sitting on a low table beside his chair, but appeared to be untouched. Doom saw me glance at the glass and asked. "Can I get you a drink, Charlie?"

"Didn't anyone ever tell you about Injuns?" I asked. "If it wasn't for booze, your people would still be trying to battle their way off the boat at Plymouth Rock!"

Teller snorted and Doom raised an eyebrow, but made a rapid recovery. "I'm sorry. I'd forgotten you don't drink."

We all sat down and I leaned back in the overstuffed chair, waiting. Doom glanced at me, while Teller went back to staring out the window.

"Mr. Teller has a problem," Doom stated rather delicately. "Simon, maybe you'd better explain. You haven't said much until now."

Teller reached for the drink, then seemed to think better of the move. He leaned away from the window to half face us. "It involves my wife," he said. "I think she's being blackmailed."

*   *   *

It wasn't until the next day that I learned a good deal more about his wife, Toni. I got some information after I called Sam Light's office and asked him to run copies of stories on the Tellers. From the newsclippings, I learned Simon Teller was in his sixties and Toni in her late thirties. Neither had ever been married when they met at some charity function. It wasn't long before they were wed, and from all reports, they were exceedingly happy during their five years of marriage. Three years ago, they even went so far as to adopt a young boy they named Brian. But I didn't know this as the three of us sat beside the window and Teller expounded on his belief.

"Toni has always been conservative in her personal habits," Teller stated slowly, scowling as he chose his words. "Recently, though, she has been drinking more than is good for anyone, and she's taking prescription pills to sleep. I think she's on the verge of a nervous breakdown."

"There must be more to it than that," Doom suggested quietly. It was probably fifteen seconds before Simon Teller nodded.

"By accident, I happened to learn that over the last six months Toni has withdrawn all of the money out of her personal savings account. In addition, a pair of diamond earrings I gave her as a fifth wedding anniversary present have disappeared." He paused for a moment, shaking his head, as though trying to understand. "When I suggested they were stolen and that we should notify the police, she reacted strangely. Finally, she told me she lost the earrings at a party and had not wanted to tell me."

"She lost *both* earrings at a party?" I asked. Doom nodded as I spoke. He was mulling the same question.

"It didn't sound logical," Teller agreed. "That's why I'm here. I want to know who's blackmailing her."

"Well, first we'll have to learn why she's in trouble," Doom stated. "We may have to look at her life before she met you."

"No!" Simon Teller's tone was like a gunshot as he arose full height from his chair. "I won't have that! I don't want to know why, I simply want to know who! I don't want you digging up old bones that might develop into any kind of scandal for those garish tabloids, understand?"

"If we turn up the blackmailer, Mr. Teller, what do you intend to do about it?" Doom asked quietly. I knew what he was thinking: that Teller might go after him or her with a gun. It's happened.

The business executive shook his head, still standing. "My wife is under enough stress without getting a lot of negative, unwanted publicity," he explained. "I want to know who is causing the problem, and I'll handle them without bringing the police into the matter." He glanced at Doom, then at me, trying to determine whether we would cooperate.

"I think we can handle things that way," Doom said, with a slight frown. "But it's imperative that I talk to your wife."

Teller started to shake his head, but Doom went on before the client could protest vocally. "Tell her I'm investigating somebody at your plant and I'm coming over to report. You can be too busy to see me immediately, which will give me a chance to size her up. I'd like to do it tomorrow."

"I don't know," Teller growled. "She's not stupid, you know."

"I just want to get my own feeling for where she's at," Doom explained. After a moment, Simon Teller nodded agreement.

"Just remember what I said," he growled, as Jonathon Doom was showing him out. "I don't want to know why. I want to know *who!*"

With Simon Teller gone, Doom mixed himself a drink and made me a cup of coffee. While he was doing that, I glanced around the room. It was typical Southern California, with big windows and lots of light. The furnishings were modern but comfortable.

"What do you pay for rent in a place like this?" I asked as he brought my coffee. You have to understand that I never went to charm school. I was brought up on the rather simple premise that if you don't ask, you don't learn.

"I don't pay rent," Doom said, taking the chair Teller had left. "I own the building."

"Oh!" That settled that. "I gather I'm already on your payroll. How much are you paying me?"

He settled back in his chair, drink in hand, and surveyed me coolly. Suddenly, I felt a bit silly in my Western-style dress. It was hardly the uniform for haggling. Problem was, this was the dress I liked and preferred.

"How much do you get for falling a horse?" Doom

wanted to know. "What's the average pay for a tough stunt?"

"Well, there are some minimums, and after that you negotiate with the producer," I explained. "I usually get about three hundred for one fall. If the horse is supposed to rear and go over backwards, I hope to get out of the saddle without being maimed. I get at least seven-fifty for that. Usually more."

"And when was the last time you did that kind of stunt?" Doom demanded. I hesitated before answering. It was a rather lame reply.

"Maybe a year," I admitted. It had been closer to two. "All the producers seem to favor multiple car crashes for excitement these days."

That brought an understanding nod. Doom obviously kept track of what was happening in the film and television business. He paused, considering for a moment, then looked at me.

"Well, Charlie, I'm prepared to start you at six hundred a week until we find out whether this arrangement is going to work. How does that sound?"

"Pretty good," I agreed. "But there may be a conflict of interest."

"How so?" He was looking out the window as though not really interested.

"Sam Light and I are pretty close. If we get involved in any big headline-type stories, I'll want to talk to him. Give him the stories first."

I expected an argument on that point, but the former actor chuckled, still looking out the window. "That'd sort of be like having a top press agent I didn't have to pay, wouldn't it?"

Before I could agree, the doorbell rang and I rose without thinking. Doom waved his hand in the direction of the door. "Would you get that, Charlie? It's probably that investigator from the district attorney's office."

I crossed the carpet and opened the door. It was no investigator. It was a woman, who seemed close to tears.

"I have to see Mr. Doom!" she stated, voice catching in her throat. I'd never been an official door-opener before. I wasn't sure how I was supposed to handle this. She was a nice-looking lady, probably in her mid-twenties. She wore a coat, so I couldn't really get a good idea of her build, but her face was beautiful.

"Do you have an appointment?" I asked, while taking all of this in.

"No, but I have to see him!" That catch was still in her tone, and she frowned at me as though I was a threat of some kind. "It's a matter of life and death—mine!"

"Let her in, Charlie," Doom ordered from somewhere behind me.

Chapter Four

The woman looked past me, still frowning, but with signs of recognition. "You really *are* Jonathon Doom!" Her tone was one of awe mixed with accusation. Not knowing what to expect, I stepped back to allow her to meet Doom in the middle of the floor. "I need your help."

Jonathon fell right into the character he had played all those years on the tube. He reached out and took both of her hands, holding them as he looked into her troubled face. When he spoke, his tone was soothing and filled with concern.

"You mentioned a matter of life and death."

The woman nodded. "Someone's trying to kill me. A truck ran into my car."

"This is a large city, miss." He shook his head as

27

he said it, tone still soothing. "Do you know how many collisions there are in Los Angeles every day?"

I didn't know how many and figured he didn't, either. We both knew there were dozens, but this would probably not impress our visitor.

"Try to understand!" Her voice was demanding, yet pleading. "When I was helped out of the wreckage, the other driver had disappeared. And the cops said the truck had been stolen three hours earlier."

Doom glanced at me, his eyes showing interest; then his gaze went back to the woman's face. "What did you say your name was, miss?"

"I didn't." Her tone was suddenly brusque, and she stiffened with caution at Doom's question. Standing by, watching, I could see his interest growing. I was wondering what you do with two clients at once. This had never happened on his TV show. His tone was still soothing and reasonable, but Doom had released his comforting hold on her hands.

"If the truck was stolen, the driver would hardly stick around." He hesitated, then went on before she could interrupt. "But if your suspicions are correct, there's usually a motive. Why would someone want you dead?"

She looked as though she was about to reply, when the doorbell sounded again. Doom glanced toward the door.

"That'll be the lieutenant," Doom stated. "Please let him in, Charlie."

Sidney Brock hadn't changed much in the five years since I'd seen him. His face had sagged a little, and when he took off his hat, there was considerable graying. He stared at me, trying to remember where we had connected. I could see the front-and-side police mug book photos flipping through his mind.

"Good afternoon, Mr. Brock. I'm Charlie Cougar." Brock nodded, suddenly remembering me.

"That's *Lieutenant* Brock," he rasped. Then he stepped past me, interested in the pair in the center of the floor.

"Well, Mrs. Jensen, this is hardly a place I'd expect to find you," Brock stated, staring at the woman. If I know what the word dismay means, I think it fit her at that moment. She spoke hurriedly, her added nervousness in her voice.

"I was just leaving." She glanced at my new boss. "Sorry to burst in, Mr. Doom. I'll be in touch again." She ignored Brock, heading for the door, and I stepped ahead of her to open it. If this job fizzled out, I was thinking, maybe I could get a job as a hotel doorman.

"No problem," Doom called after her. "Give me a call. You must have my number!" But she was already closing the door as he spoke.

"What did she want?" Brock demanded. He had rotated on his axis to watch her leave, but now he turned back to Jonathon Doom. The latter offered him a condescending smile.

"I have no idea, Sid. You frightened her away before she could tell me."

"Maybe she's part of the reason I'm here," Brock declared, reaching into his shirt pocket. He pulled out a scrap torn from a printed page. It looked like ordinary newsprint. "The District Attorney is interested in knowing what this is all about!"

"It's exactly what it says," Doom told him quietly. "It's all there in the ad." I moved beside him for moral support, or whatever else was needed. I realized I never had liked Brock. Doom handed me the bit of paper, which turned out to be an ordinary classified advertisement probably torn out of the *Los Angeles Times*.

It was laid out like a business card, the copy reading:

TROUBLE, INCORPORATED
Confidential Inquiries
Jonathon Doom

Doom's phone number was listed in the right-hand corner.

"Well, the D.A. seems to think you're playing private eye without a license," Brock accused. "And you must be up to something, if Linda Jensen's trying to hire you!"

Doom raised his left eyebrow exactly as he had done at least once in every one of the old shows. "Linda Jensen?"

"I don't know what name she gave you, but that was Linda Jensen. The mask and the 'Scarlet Canary' tag she's hiding behind haven't fooled any of us for a minute. She was spotted the minute she crossed the county line!"

I was certain Doom had known who she was from the start, but I thought I'd give him some breathing time. I put in my two cents' worth, hoping for more information.

"I thought I recognized her from the old newspaper photos, Mr. Doom. She was Guns Jensen's wife. Tied the knot with him just before he went to trial so she wouldn't be able to testify against him. Didn't help, though. He was convicted of murder."

"I remember now." Doom was frowning as he nodded his head slowly. "He ended up on Death Row, and she divorced him soon after he was convicted."

I nodded in agreement. "That's the way I remember it. I saw on the news that he's been brought back to L.A. for an appeal of his case."

Brock glared at me. "You were a pretty good stuntman five years ago," he admitted. "How can you stand playing straight man to someone with a name like Leonard Squiglemayr?"

I returned the glare. "I'm still a pretty good stuntman if you'd like to try a couple of falls," I suggested. "Mr. Doom's doing okay by me." I wasn't even sure what this was all about, but it seemed like Doom needed someone backing his play. "What're you doing here, by the way?"

"He's an errand boy for the district attorney," Doom said quietly, not able to hide a slight smile.

"You'll always be Lenny Squiglemayr to me!" Brock declared, glaring at him. In fact, if men could spit their words, that's what he did. He tried to follow it with a laugh, but it didn't quite come off. "That judge was crazy to let you change your name legally. Now you're a phony private eye with some kind of show biz razzle-dazzle gimmick!"

"I am not a private detective," Doom said quietly. "I listen to people's problems and try to help them.

You should go home and read some of the old TV scripts, if you still have them.

"As for the name, no one could remember my name when it was Squiglemayr. As Jonathon Doom, I think I'll be able to help enough people to make it worth my while." He paused for a moment, then asked with patent politeness, "Is that all, Sidney?"

"That's not all by a long shot!" the other growled. "We'll be watching you." He turned, pulled his felt hat down hard on his head and marched to the door. He didn't even look back before he slammed it.

"What was that all about?" I wanted to know, still staring at the door.

"We may never know. He just called and said he had to see me," was Doom's reply. "Actually, I think he expected to get the job you're doing!"

It made some sort of sense, I guess. Sid Brock had been a member of the Los Angeles County Sheriff's Department in the days when we were doing the *Trouble, Incorporated* show. Somehow, he got signed on to moonlight as a technical advisor regarding weapons use and the ins and outs of law enforcement. Some of his technical advice was out of the Sidney Brock book of justice, instead of the true laws that govern Los Angeles.

The sheriff took notice and had a meeting with Jonathon Doom and the show's writers. When he learned Brock was the source of the goofs, he arranged to have his deputy pulled off the show and put to work as a jailer. Brock had eventually quit the department and come to Doom, wanting the tech job back. When Doom refused, that was it.

"What's he doing for the D.A.?" I wanted to know. Again, Doom shook his head, slightly amused.

"Harassing me, I think."

"And what's all this double-talk about a red canary or something? He lost me on that."

Doom didn't answer immediately. Instead, he bent over the morning paper, separating the sections until he found what he wanted. He folded back a page and handed it to me. "Take a look at this and you'll know as much as I do."

It was a four-color advertisement with big bold type, but that didn't detract from the photo of a young woman in a low-cut gown. She stood before a microphone, arms spread in the familiar gesture of one belting out a song. The body was something to see, but most of her face was covered by a concealing but delicately cut mask. Like her gown, the mask was a flaming shade of red.

I stared at the photo closely, making comparisons from what I could see of her features. "Looks like the girl that just left here."

Doom simply nodded and I went back to reading the type surrounding the photograph

WHO IS THE SCARLET CANARY?

**The Mystery Girl of Music
Meet America's Fastest Rising Songstress!
Hear This New Sensation!
Friday 8 p.m.**

The advertisement carried the logo and channel of a local independent radio station.

"It has to be the same girl," I announced, still eyeing the ad. "She had that coat on, but I couldn't mistake that figure. Why the mask?"

Doom looked over my shoulder at the ad. He shook his head with a frown. "It's probably just a publicity gimmick. I heard somewhere that the show's producer has insured her voice for a million dollars! Then again, she may not want the old mob to know she's back in town."

"What do you think?"

"I think we'd better ask her. If we don't hear from her, we'll go after her at the show." He heaved a sigh. "Meantime, that brings us back to Simon Teller and his wife's blackmailer."

"What about a price for all this?" I asked. That brought an amused smile from Doom.

"Mr. Teller and I discussed that before you arrived," he said quietly. "You don't want to know the cost to him, Charlie. Not yet, at least."

I nodded. "You're telling me it's none of my business."

"Well, I wouldn't put it quite that way," he said, "but you've got the general idea."

"Is there anything I should be doing immediately?"

Doom shook his head. "Not until after I talk to Toni Teller. We've met a number of times on a social level, but I don't know just how much I'm going to get out of her." He was struck by a sudden thought. "If you talk to your friend Sam Light, you can't tell him what's gone on here this morning. Maybe later, but certainly not at this point."

I nodded my understanding of the ground rules. Rather than talking to Sam, I was much more interested in telling Sue Tallfeather I was out of the process-serving business.

Chapter Five

Back at the Heartbreak Hotel, I called Sue Tall-feather. I got her voice mail instead. Much as I hate those things, I tried to sound happy about talking to a machine. I told her I had a new job and that I'd stop by that night to tell her about it. She'd be at work, I knew, but she was supposed to get a break around ten o'clock.

After a moment, I called the Screen Actors Guild, then the Stuntmen's Association to see whether anyone was in need of my talents. The standard answers are "Nothing today, sorry" and "Call later."

I was just about to get in the shower when Georgie called. "I'm at Columbia's prop department." He sounded disheartened rather than excited. "The balsa limb and the hardware're on my truck."

"What's the problem?" I wanted to know.

"They've changed the schedule," he said. "I don't know when I'm supposed t'do this gag."

"Is there anyone in their office?"

"Not now," Georgie replied. "I tried to call. No answer."

"There's not much you can do except sit tight, Georgie. They're probably out trying to find enough loot to finish the picture."

"Great!" he muttered into my ear. "What am I supposed t'do with the stuff on my truck?"

"Either store it in your garage until you get news or take it back to Columbia." I knew how he felt, I'd been there. When you're getting started in the business, you take what you can get. I'd been on several shows that were never finished and I never got paid. It happens. In fact, it happens too often. Stuntmen don't have agents; they have to fend for themselves.

Georgie muttered a dispirited thanks and hung up. I settled back on my bed and inspected the toes of my boots, which had gotten scuffed during the course of the day. I took them off and found my moccasins under the edge of the bed, slipping them on.

I took the stairs down to the lobby, checked for messages, and walked the eight blocks to the gym. Keeping fit goes with the kind of work I do, and being on Doom's payroll wasn't reason enough to get lazy.

I don't know who owned the place, but it was managed by Alma Roberts, a woman in her mid-fifties who wasn't afraid to let her hair show its gray. She had been a stunt double for some top female stars until her reflexes began to slow and she knew it was time to quit. She'd gotten the job at the gym, where she not only managed but spent enough time with the equipment to maintain the figure of a twenty-year-old.

She greeted me as I came in and I gave her a hug, before I went into the locker room to change. I watched several guys I knew well enough to exchange nods with before I started some stretching exercises. Then I got on a board and did a hundred sit-ups followed by my usual hundred push-ups. I also worked a bit with the weights, but more as a matter of maintaining strength than building muscle. A muscle-bound stuntman tends to be awkward, and gets in his own way.

I showered at the gym and made it back to the hotel. Frankly, I would hate exercise were it not for the fact that I feel better when it's over. On that note, I wondered what I was going to do until I could see Sue Tallfeather.

A bit over a century ago, Sue and I probably would have been tribal enemies. Her Sioux ancestors were settling accounts with General Sherman and the Seventh Cavalry at Little Big Horn about the same time mine were riding with Geronimo to terrorize the settlers of the Southwest. My Apache people occasionally teamed up with the Comanches for attacks upon the white settlers or in efforts to steal their horses, but we had little to do with other tribes, except to try to kill them.

That bit of history may have had something to do with the chemistry between Sue and myself. We liked each other, but there remained a gulf that was more than tribal. She had been born in Los Angeles, and had all the aspects of what we call an Apple Indian— red on the outside, white on the inside.

At the other extreme, I was brought up on the reservation and trained to believe in most of the taboos and legends of my people—even some of the superstitions. Sue was pursuing a degree in computer science and seemed to feel I should be concentrating on more cerebral pursuits than the physical ones I had worked in to date. What it all came down to was that we were more than platonic friends, but not quite married.

This was why I wanted to brief her on my work with Jonathon Doom. She didn't disapprove of my using my knowledge of courts and law enforcement to work part-time for Sam Light, but she definitely disapproved of my efforts as a process server. Her attitude was that most people had troubles enough without being dragged into court. As nearly as I could figure, she saw me as an evil force that helped get people in front of a judge. I wouldn't say it to her, of course, but I had a hunch she had her own superstitions, even though she did her best not to recognize or acknowledge them.

As for the process-serving gig, I hadn't cared for it either, until I managed to put it in context with being an Indian. I made a game out of it. I was the wily Apache tracking the enemy. The fact that my environment was a lot of freeways and tall buildings rather than an Arizona desert made the game a bit difficult at times, but it managed to keep me amused and focused during such efforts.

Some of us Indians have a philosophy that seems

to work: Never stand when you can sit; never sit when you can lie down. I closed the drapes to keep out the sun and had no problem falling asleep.

My mental alarm clock woke me at eight-thirty. I washed the sleep off my face, straightened my clothes and pulled on my moccasins. My body told me I needed protein before I ventured too far.

As I passed the front desk, the clerk held up a pink telephone message slip. I crossed to take it and learned that Doom wanted me to meet him at his place the next morning at nine. He wanted me to accompany him to the Teller residence to interview the wife.

Chapter Six

The coffee shop that serves the hotel was half empty. I walked in, pondering why Jonathon Doom would want me along for his interview with Toni Teller. Looking half asleep, Bob the Burglar sat at the counter staring fixedly at the bottom of an empty cup. Bob has a Czech last name of about sixteen syllables that no one but he can pronounce. He had done time for burglary in one of California's incarceration palaces, hence his accepted handle: Bob the Burglar. These days, though, he was on his best behavior. A thoroughly professional electrician when sober, he had a job at Columbia Pictures.

"You need a refill?" I asked him. He looked up abruptly, grinning. There was a gap between his teeth that I thought needed the attention of a good dentist, but the girls adored it. I had hired him a couple of times when I was trying to serve reluctant people with a court summons.

"Naw," he answered. "I was just thinking about goin' to that AA meeting down at the church. You wanna go?"

I shook my head. "I have an appointment a little later and I need something in my stomach."

Bob looked me up and down, then asked, "What've you been doin'?"

"Looking for work." I looked him in the eye. "How're you doing on the program?"

Bob the Burglar cast me another grin. "Piece of cake. I've been sober for almost six months."

"Don't get over-confident," I told him. "It's easy to do."

"Not likely," he declared. "All I hafta do is remember my last hangover." He slid off the stool and stood erect. "I don't wanna be late. See you." He waved a hand and I watched as he strode out the door and down Hollywood Boulevard toward the meeting site.

I had taken Bob to his first Alcoholics Anonymous meeting, where an old-timer had volunteered to be his sponsor. That meant offering advice, listening to problems and even holding a guy's hand, if that's what it took to keep him sober through the periodic downturns most of us experience early on. The only thing a good sponsor will not do is loan a recovering alcoholic money.

I ordered a bowl of chili and thought about Bob's bad old days and some of my own as I ate food that was spiced with Mexican hot peppers. My forehead was dotted with perspiration when done, but I felt better. I downed my coffee and stopped at the hotel desk to see whether there were any messages. None. The Heartbreak Hotel is old-fashioned enough that it still has dial telephones and none of those red lights to tell you of a waiting message.

Back in my room, I called Sam Light's number and got his answering machine. I gave him a fast, three-minute account of my meeting with Doom, leaving out the parts about the two clients. I just wanted him to know I had followed up on the job tip and appreciated it.

To help finance her education, Sue Tallfeather worked three evenings a week as a waitress in a bowling alley in the San Fernando Valley. I had first met her there when I invaded the place to serve a construction worker with a summons.

Her normal hours were from six in the evening until two, but if business was slow, they often closed early. I was hoping that would be the case on this night. I wanted to be alone with Sue, not surrounded by a bunch of people.

I sat at the rickety round table I called my office and made notes on what had happened that day. It was a kind of log I kept in case I had to refresh my memory later. I had learned that much from Danny Dark, who had run the process-serving agency before he met his end. But that's another story.

I tried Sam Light again, and got the same taped message. I hung up the phone, pondering. Maybe he was in San Francisco. He hadn't said much, but I knew there was a girl there who seemed determined to prove to him that absence does not make the heart grow fonder. I had never met her, and all I knew was that her name was Carol. Sam had found her in the Mojave Desert and had taken her to San Francisco with him. She'd spent most of her life in a dusty little town and, according to Sam, was having a lot of fun dating other guys while he was slaving in Los Angeles to rebuild his career. Light was not one to let his hair down, and when he quietly explained to me what was happening, I knew he was hurting bad.

I killed some more time by wiping and polishing my Tony Lama boots. Finally, it was ten o'clock and I didn't wait any longer.

In my truck, I herded the steer horns in front of me through the concrete canyons of Hollywood and up onto the freeway that led into the Valley. I was soon sliding into a spot in the bowling alley's parking lot. Most of the lot was empty, which I took as a good sign. Maybe they were closing early.

The name of the place was The Warbonnet, and Sue fit right in. She was dressed in a long-sleeved dress of purple velvet that ended at her knees, and her feet were clad in beaded buckskin moccasins. Her waist held a belt beaded in the same pattern. The braids dangling on each side of her face were decorated with beaded buckskin holders. She certainly represented the name of the place!

Only three of the bowling lanes were in operation, and the girl running the snack bar was starting to close down—another good sign. I ordered a cup of coffee before she dumped the pot, and Sue spotted me sliding into a booth. She offered an acknowledging smile and a nod, since both of her hands were carrying a tray.

I was halfway through the coffee when Sue deposited her empty tray and came over to sit down across from me.

"Slow night?" I asked. She nodded with a slight frown.

"Slow tips, too," she said.

"Good days and bad days," I reminded her. That was the philosophy she had fed me about her work.

"It's been slow all week," she said. "I may have to find another job if this keeps up."

"Maybe I can get you one with Jonathon Doom," I suggested, not really meaning it, just trying to open the subject. Her frown deepened.

"Who?"

"You're not old enough to have watched a show called *Trouble, Incorporated*? The lead was a guy named Jonathon Doom."

She shook her head. "Okay. You have me properly confused. Tell me what you're talking about."

"It was a TV show a few years back. Jonathon Doom made a career of helping people in trouble who couldn't go to the cops."

"I don't think I've ever seen it."

"Well, Jonathon Doom is a real person, and he's set himself up in business to help people. I've just signed on as his assistant." I tried to keep the excitement out of my voice. I wanted her to be pleased. "What do you think?"

"Did this fellow have an assistant in the series?" she wanted to know.

I nodded. "Yeah, he did."

"Maybe I should look at a couple of the shows before I give you an answer." She was still frowning, but somewhere behind the expression, I thought I saw laughter in her eyes.

"The guy was a clod," I told her. "Doom's promised me I don't have to be as stupid as the writers made his assistant."

That made her laugh as she leaned over the table. "Tell me about it."

"Well, he got his first two clients during our meeting," I told her. "One was a guy who thinks his wife is being blackmailed. The other was a woman who thinks someone's trying to kill her."

Sue was frowning again. She shook her head. "I'm not sure I'm going to like this, Charlie. It sounds like you could get hurt. Are you sure you haven't been hired for your muscle?"

I offered a sigh. "Sue, I'm no brain trust. I'm a simple Injun who does physical work to make a living. You have to agree that working with Doom is better than shoving legal papers at people who don't want them, having horses fall on me, or being put out of business by a dog's tombstone!"

She thought for a moment and finally nodded. "I guess it does sound a bit safer." She glanced toward her last table and started to rise. "I have to see if they need anything else."

"How late'll you be here?" I asked hopefully. Her smile revealed white, even teeth. She offered a shrug.

"I'll ask Joe what he thinks," she promised, turning away. A few moments later, she was back, smiling.

"He's closing up as soon as those guys quit horsing around."

"Then let's go!" I was struggling to get out of the booth without turning over the table. I'm not clumsy, but I do get excited. "Let's go up on the ridge and watch the lights."

"Sounds good," she agreed. There was sudden silence from the bowlers as we walked behind their position and made for the door. They were all looking at us, and I couldn't help offering a grin. Sort of a way of letting them know that sometimes the redman wins.

We found a spot on the reverse slope of the Hollywood Hills that looks out over the lights of the San Fernando Valley. So far, this particular spot had not yet been cluttered up with houses. I pulled the truck into it and cut off the engine before turning to Sue, staring at her. She returned the stare, puzzled.

"What's wrong?" she wanted to know. "What are you looking at?"

"Just wondering whether I should kiss you now or later."

She laughed and spread her arms. "Now, idiot!"

The radio was playing soft music from the Forties, and we might still have been there had the music not suddenly stopped.

"This is a news flash! The Los Angeles County sheriff's office has just reported that Larry 'Guns' Jensen has escaped from custody. He is dangerous and may be armed, law enforcement sources say. The convicted killer has been on San Quentin's death row for the past two years, awaiting execution. He had been transferred to the Los Angeles County Jail in connection with an appeal of his death sentence.

"There is little other news at this time, but it has been revealed that Jensen was visited in the county jail by his former wife, Linda Jensen, early this morning. Further details will be announced as we receive them."

I was kissing Sue as the news flash started, but then I pulled away, staring at the radio. When the music started again, I glanced at Sue Tallfeather. Her expression was one of puzzlement, and her eyes reflected hurt.

Chapter Seven

I returned her stare for a moment, then told her about Linda Jensen's unannounced appearance at Jonathon Doom's apartment. "She didn't tell us she had been to see Guns before she came to us," I told her, as the tag to the explanation.

"From the sound of things, she didn't have a chance," Sue commented. The look of hurt was gone, but she still frowned, now in concentration. "The man from the district attorney's office scared her off."

I nodded agreement. "Sounds like it, doesn't it?"

"It seems to me you're getting mixed up with gangsters and killers again." She shook her head. "I'm not sure you weren't better off chasing people across pet graveyards."

It was my turn to frown. "I'm not in any danger. Fact is, I don't think she'll ever come back."

Sue glanced down at the clock on my dashboard, noting that it was almost midnight. She heaved a sigh. "I have an early class tomorrow, Charlie. You'd better take me back."

I hesitated, thinking about the romance that the news flash had destroyed. I knew there was no point in trying to reestablish that now. "Yeah," I finally agreed. "I guess you're right."

I drove her back to The Warbonnet parking lot with an empty feeling in my stomach. I got out and followed her to her car. Like the gentleman I tried to be, I unlocked it for her and opened the door. She turned to me for a kiss, then offered me a smile.

"I'm sorry, Charlie. There'll be other nights."

"I hope so." I closed the door and stood back as she started the car and circled out of the lot. I had a feeling I was like Sam Light—I was losing something, too.

I didn't sleep well that night, and arrived at Jonathon Doom's door about eight-thirty. He was still in his dressing gown, with a cup of coffee in his hand, as he let me in. As he closed the door, he pointed toward the kitchen. "There's coffee and rolls in there. Let me finish my morning chores."

His shower was going full blast while I drank coffee and looked at the front page of the *Los Angeles Times*, which lay on the kitchen table. The story about Guns Jensen's escape made headlines, but the story didn't reveal any more than I had heard on the news flash the night before. In fact, the *Times* didn't even have the bit about Jensen's ex-wife visiting him earlier in the day.

By the time I finished the cup of black coffee, Doom was coming out of his bedroom, dressed in an expensive suit. He looked me up and down critically. What he saw was a Western-cut shirt, black Levis, a matching silver and turquoise buckle and bolo, polished cowboy boots, and my cowboy hat.

"I have a jacket in my truck," I told him. He kept frowning at the hat. "Okay, I'll take the eagle feather out of the band."

"That'll have to do," he replied. I hoped he didn't have ideas about remaking me in his image.

"What's the plan for today?" I asked him.

"First, we're going to see Toni Teller. You can ride with me and I'll bring you back here."

We were well on the way to the Teller mansion when Doom asked, "Did you see the story about Guns Jensen in the *Times*?"

"I read it while you were in the shower. Didn't say much. They didn't even have the bit about his wife visiting him."

Doom turned to look at me and almost hit a yellow convertible pulling away from the curb ahead of us. "What visit?"

"You must have gone to bed early. I heard it on a news flash just before midnight. They announced Guns had busted out after his ex-wife visited him earlier in jail."

Doom hadn't even noticed the convertible. Or, if he did, he ignored it. His attention was back on the street as he shook his head slowly. His eyes were narrowed in thought, a ploy he had used on his TV show. "Then she visited him before she came to us. It's no wonder Brock wondered why she was seeing me!"

"I'm sure the D.A. heard about her visit before she was out the jailhouse door." I glanced at him. "Any idea what's going on?"

Doom shook his head, again irritated that he had to make the admission. "Not the faintest."

The Teller mansion was set back from the street, and it was surrounded by a great number of well-manicured homes. The location alone was worth several fortunes. An electronically controlled gate blocked the driveway, and Doom announced himself to the microphone. No one answered, but the gate opened almost immediately, swinging back on well-oiled hinges. As we drove through, I glanced in the side mirror and noted that it immediately swung back to a locked position.

The house was semi-traditional Spanish style, employing red tile for roofing and glaring white stucco that made one realize why sunglasses sell so well in Southern California. We pulled up to the parking area in front of the house, and I followed Doom up the polished granite steps to the door. He rang the bell, which I could hear chiming throughout the house. In a moment, the door was opened by a young woman wearing a maid's uniform.

"Yes?" she asked, her left eyebrow arched as if to indicate she was in charge and wanted us to know it. I also detected a slight curl of the lip, as she inspected my two-tone, embroidered boots.

"I'm Jonathon Doom," the boss replied, arching his

own brow to let her know she should have known who he was and that he was coming. "We have an appointment with Mr. Teller."

She opened the door a bit and allowed us to enter. She seemed about nineteen or twenty, and judging from her accent, she had still been in Mexico when my boss was making weekly appearances on the tube. No wonder she didn't know who he was. She closed the door and led us down a long hallway of Italian marble. She halted at a heavy mahogany door, knocked twice, then opened it.

"Señor Doom and another hombre to see you, El Jefe Teller," she announced. Instead of swinging the door back to enter, she pushed it to allow Teller to frame himself and look over her shoulder. He had a cordless telephone in his hand and a scowl on his face.

"Just a minute, Joe," he said into the phone and lowered it, looking at Doom. "I'm in the middle of an important call right now, Jonathon." His eyes switched to the maid. "Take them into the parlor, Maria, and ask my wife to entertain them for a few minutes."

"Si, señor." We went back down the hallway to another mahogany door, which she opened and motioned us through. She paused, looking toward the couch on which Toni Teller was sitting. Beside her was a child of perhaps six. She seemed to have been reading to him from a book, but looked up in surprise as we entered and paused.

"El Jefe asked that you entertain these gentlemen for a few minutes," the maid explained. "He is on an overseas call."

"All right, Maria. I'll take care of it." Toni Teller gave the book to the child and rose to face us, frowning. "I'm sorry, gentlemen. I wasn't aware we were having guests this early."

"We have some business with your husband, Mrs. Teller," Doom said. "I'm Jonathan Doom, and this is my assistant, Mr. Cougar."

She indicated a pair of chairs across from the coffee table. "Please sit down. I'm sure Simon won't keep you waiting any longer than necessary."

Doom seemed perfectly at home as he settled into the overstuffed chair. I edged myself onto the other one, sinking into it in spite of my care. I don't trust chairs that make me feel like I'm in the center of a cocoon. I get a trapped feeling verging on claustrophobia.

"I remember you, Mr. Doom," Toni Teller said, offering him a smile. But it was only the lips that were smiling; her eyes were judging him carefully, wondering why he was in her house. "I think I saw every show in your series."

Jonathon seemed to bask, leaning forward to face her with a gracious smile. "I'm surprised you remember."

"Read to me, Mommy," the little boy whined, shoving the book back in her lap. He seemed small for his age and was pale-skinned, with blond hair. He needed some time in the sun.

"I can't right now," the woman declared, reaching for an electronic pad that featured several buttons. She punched one. "I'll have Miss Boyd read to you."

"Not her. *You*, Mommy," the child insisted, kicking his heels against the front of the sofa.

"You have to understand, Brian." Toni Teller was

uptight, but she tried to keep her tone reasonable. "I have to talk to these gentlemen."

Suddenly, the woman was in tears, gathering the boy to her and hugging him. Doom and I glanced at each other, wondering what had brought this on.

"Yes, ma'am?" a contralto voice sounded behind us. Doom and I both turned to look at the tall, efficient-looking blond woman who had come into the room. She was dressed in a white nurse's uniform, complete with peaked cap. There was no makeup beyond a bit of lipstick, and her hair was done up in a tight bun.

"I need for you to take Brian to his room and read to him," Toni Teller stated, rubbing her eyes to wipe away the tears. She watched as the nurse, poker-faced, came across the room and took the crying boy out of his mother's arms.

"I have some tranquilizers, Mrs. Teller. I'll bring you one, if you like." Her tone was even and professional.

"Don't bother!" Toni snapped, glaring at the nurse. She turned and stalked out of the room, holding the boy.

"I'm sorry you had to see this," she announced, turning back to us. "I've been rather upset lately."

"That's obvious," Doom told her. "I think you should see a doctor. Someone who can help relieve your tensions."

"I'm just worried," the woman stated. "Brian's adopted. We've never told him, but one of his schoolmates has. Now he's confused and thinks he's different from other children. I don't know what to do."

Doom thought about it for a moment, then nodded.

"Since he already knows he's adopted, that's not a problem. Why don't you point out to him that other parents have to take what they get, but you and Simon had the chance to look all over the country and he's the one you chose. That makes him special. He's the one you brought home to love."

Toni Teller stared at Doom for a moment, then rose suddenly, breaking into tears again. She rushed out of the room, as Doom and I stood up, watching her. An instant later, Simon Teller was in the doorway, looking after his wife whose retreating footsteps could be heard on the tile floor.

Slowly, Teller entered and closed the door, staring at one of us, then the other. Finally, he came over and settled on the vacated couch as we returned to the chairs.

"I think you now have some indication of the problem here," he stated, his expression showing some of the misery he had to be feeling.

"She says her problem is the fact that another kid told Brian he's adopted," Doom said, watching his client closely. "I think there's a great deal more to her troubles than that."

Teller nodded, "So do I, but I can do nothing about it until I know who is involved. That's what I want you to learn."

Doom asked Teller how long his wife had been disturbed. The answer was, about six months.

Doom asked for the name of the orphanage where they had found little Brian. I didn't hear Teller's reply clearly, but Doom made a note on the pad he drew from an inside pocket.

"Again, remember that I don't want to know why. I want to know *who* it is that's blackmailing her," Teller announced. He stood abruptly to announce that the meeting was over.

"What's the name of the boy's nurse?" Doom asked suddenly, as we neared the door.

"Helen Boyd." Teller added, "Toni hired her. She appears to be very good at what she does."

Back in the car and past the security gate, Doom remained silent, apparently deep in thought. As he drew into the parking lot behind his building, he turned to look at me.

"We should have taken both cars. We could have saved a good deal of time." He paused, then motioned to indicate my truck on the far side of the lot. "I want you to go to the Wayside Foundling Home and learn what you can about Brian Teller's life before he was adopted."

"Chances are they aren't going to tell me much," I argued. "They may have to call Teller to verify it's okay to give me information. And I'm not sure he wants us digging that deep. Besides, where is it?"

"Look it up in the phone book," Doom instructed, getting out of the car. I got out, waved at him as I headed for my truck. I didn't remember any of the cases in the old TV series having the complications we were facing.

I found a Denny's coffee shop and took two parking spaces so that no one could damage the steer horns on the front of the truck. Not accidentally, at least. While I was waiting for my order, I found the phone booth and went through three volumes of the Los Angeles County directory before I found a listing for the Wayside Foundling Home in Covina, about thirty miles down the social scale from Beverly Hills.

I downed my meal without really tasting it. I knew Covina was a sprawling bedroom community, composed of single-family homes, condos, and apartment houses peopled by commuters. A lot of its residents were young, single career girls. Some of them, I realized, might well find need for a foundling home.

After paying the bill, I pondered whether I should call the foundling home and decided against it. Experience as a process server had shown me that one is more likely to talk to people in person rather than get rejected by telephone. A sad but true facet of today's society.

I herded my truck out of the parking lot and down to Interstate Highway 10, which moves through the suburbs on the way to the Mojave Desert. It was about two o'clock when I finally found the Wayside establishment.

I parked in front and got out, pausing long enough to look it over. It was at the edge of a residential neighborhood and appeared to be fashioned from a pair of large, two-story frame houses that were probably built shortly after World War II by the same contractor. They were almost mirror images of one another, but had been joined together by a more recent single-story addition that seemed to be administrative offices.

I entered and found myself in a large room with a counter running across most of its width, penning in several clerks at paper-strewn desks. As I paused, one of the women glanced up, then stood and came to the counter.

"Can I help you?" she asked pleasantly. I edged up to her, removing my hat and trying to match her smile.

"My name is Charlie Cougar," I told her, "and I'm looking for some information on a child that you had here for a time before he was adopted."

The smile faded and she shook her head. "I'm sorry, but we are not at liberty to divulge such information." The way she said it made it obvious that this was a speech that had been learned and was delivered by rote.

"If that's the case, I think I'd like to see your manager," I told her. What had been a smile now downgraded to a sullen frown.

"Mr. Delgado is at lunch, I'm afraid. He has several appointments when he returns," the woman told me. I kept smiling.

"Well, you wouldn't mind, would you, if I hung around until he comes back from lunch? I really need to talk with him."

She looked me over, obviously wondering what a Native American in Western dress would have in common with her boss. Finally, she offered a shrug. "Suit yourself," she said, turning away. I don't know why, but I wished I had put the eagle feather back in my hat.

I found a chair and looked through a stack of magazines and pamphlets having to do with childcare. From some of the article titles, I wondered how people ever made it to adulthood before this type of publication came along. I was certain they hadn't found many subscribers on the reservation where I was born.

Bored, I stood up and started looking at photos on the wall. Some were of babies, but near the counter was a large framed photo that I presumed to be the staff of the foundling home. I eyed it for a moment, looking at the little man in the center I assumed was Mr. Delgado. There were several men dressed in white uniforms, as were the women. Several of the women wore the peaked caps of graduate nurses. One of them caught my attention, and I turned back to the woman who had greeted me.

"Ma'am, can I bother you for a moment?" I asked. She looked up, scowling at the interruption. Reluctantly, she stood and came to the corner of the counter where I was eyeing the photograph. I pointed to the woman who had caught my attention.

"I think I went to school with her. What's her name?"

"That's Helen Boyd. She's not here any more."

"Oh?" I did my forlorn act. "Know where I can find her? I'd love to see her."

The woman's expression went from annoyed to stubborn. She shook her head. "She left quite unexpectedly. We don't know where she went."

I shook my head, showing my disappointment. It's strange the things you can learn to do, if you hang around movie and TV studios and watch the actors closely. "How long ago did she leave?"

"I don't know, seven or eight months ago I guess."

I offered a sigh and glanced at my watch. "I have

another appointment. Please tell Mr. Delgado I'll be back to see him later."

I whirled and almost bolted through the door. I wasn't sure what it meant, but the blond Amazon in the group photo was now Brian Teller's live-in nurse!

Chapter Eight

"**I**'m sure it means something, but I don't know what," I confessed to Jonathon Doom, after I had told him about the nurse in the picture and what little I had learned at the foundling home. "I'm also pretty certain we're not going to learn much more out there. They seem to be very private."

Doom shook his head. "I don't know what it means either, and I suspect you're right about the place. I have a hunch it's one of those places that gathers young, unmarried girls who're in a family way and takes care of their medical needs in return for the baby. They then put the baby up for adoption at a highly exorbitant fee. Most of them are approved by family services investigators, of course."

"Want me to start checking out the nurse?"

"That sounds logical," he agreed, "but let's not

worry about it tonight. You might ask your friend
Light if he knows anything about Helen Boyd. It'd be
interesting to know whether she has any kind of crim-
inal record."

"To get that kind of info, I'm going to have to tell
him why we want to know. He has contacts with the
police, but he's not going to call in favors unless
there's something in it for him."

Doom considered my statement for a moment, while
I wondered whether I should feel ashamed. I was on
Doom's payroll, but my loyalty seemed to be to Sam
Light. It was like being in two camps at the same time,
and I didn't like the feeling.

"Bring him up to date," Doom finally agreed, "but
explain that this is a story that should never see print.
Will he honor that?"

I pondered for a moment before I nodded. "I think
so."

But Doom wasn't looking at me. Instead, he was
staring out the window. The sun was down and the
Beverly Hills street lights had come on. I wondered
whether he was expecting someone.

"Anything happening on the Scarlet Canary thing?"
I asked.

"Nothing. I expected her to call, but after learning
she visited Guns Jensen before she came to us, I don't
know what to think. Until that happened, I was under
the impression that some of his old gang might be after
her for some reason."

"Maybe they still are. What're we going to do about
her?"

"I'm thinking about it. It's highly possible she's decided to seek help elsewhere after coming face to face with our Lieutenant Brock." His lips twisted in distaste, as he spoke the investigator's name. "Use the phone if you want to call Light, but don't tell him anything about Linda Jensen. That's a different bit of business."

I turned toward the door, picking up my hat on the way. "I don't think this is something to discuss on the phone. A face-to-face will be better."

"Whatever works." Doom didn't seem nearly as sure of himself as in the old days, when he had a script from which to work. I couldn't help but wonder just how this attempt to establish a new career was going to work out for both of us.

I knew where Sam Light would be. He was the scheduled speaker that night at an AA meeting in North Hollywood, and he already had the floor by the time I arrived.

Sam was wrapping up his little talk when I nodded to him and took a seat in the rear of the church recreation room where this group met. He opened a period for questions. An elderly man I didn't recognize raised his hand.

"Have you ever had an urge to drink since you joined AA?"

"I think we all have the urge from time to time. It doesn't go away for a long time, if ever. In fact, I have even had a drink!"

There were murmurs in the audience. I knew of the incident and called, "You'd better tell them about it, Sam."

Light glanced back to where I sat, then offered a tight little nod. He threw his head back and stood looking at a spot somewhere over the heads of his audience.

"It was a couple of years back, down in the Mojave Desert," he said thoughtfully, almost dreamily. "A man was holding a gun on me and ordered me to drink. I was scared and I drank the two shots that he poured."

He looked down at the audience then. "He poured a third shot and I threw it at him at the same moment I dove for the gun. He was about to shoot me when the sheriff killed him from the doorway. That sheriff then suggested we both needed a drink." He shook his head. "I turned that one down."

"Bravo!" someone yelled, and there were other murmurs of approval, but Sam shook his head.

"It wasn't that simple. A lot of times since, I've wondered whether I was really that fearful. I knew the sheriff was outside the door listening. Was it a case of my wanting the drinks, lying to myself, saying I *had* to down them? I was sure the guy didn't plan to kill me in town. His car was outside in the alley. He was going to haul me out into the desert, shoot me, and dump me in a canyon. I still wake up worrying about why I took the two shots!"

There was total silence and Sam Light glanced around the hall, then nodded. "Thanks for listening."

The evening's chairman broke up the meeting, and the members began to line up at a huge coffee dispenser. Then they split into small groups, discussing what had been said, exchanging news and asking about each others' families. Sam Light strode down the aisle between the folding chairs to where I stood.

"Thanks for coming, Injun," he greeted me, squeezing my left shoulder. "Let's get some coffee."

With filled Styrofoam cups, I led the way to some chairs in a far corner. As he sat down, he took a sip of the black brew. I did the same. It wasn't great, but it would do.

"Nice talk," I told him. "What I heard of it."

He shook his head, offering a slight frown. "I don't know that I thank you for making me tell that story about what happened down there in Beale. I've never told it to anyone but you."

"Then it's time you did. Now that it's out in the open, maybe you won't continue to feel guilty about that one slip." I paused to let him think about it for a moment before I asked, "Ever hear of a woman named Helen Boyd? She's some kind of nurse."

He pondered for an instant, then shook his head. "Not that I recall."

"Doom would like to know whether she has a jail record. I told him he has to have something to trade."

Sam chuckled before saying, "I'm sure he didn't like that. You'd better tell me about it."

"Doom's protecting reputations here, Sam. It has to be off the record."

After a moment, he nodded agreement, but he still had a frown. I launched into the story of the suspected blackmail. When I was done, Light cocked his head to look at me.

"Not wanting to know why his wife is being blackmailed tells us Simon Teller *knows* why," he suggested. I nodded agreement.

"We think so, too."

"You think it's the nurse?" I offered a shrug.

"We're just trying to sort out the players at this point. But it seems a little odd that she would leave the foundling home and come to the Tellers just to take care of the kid."

Light shook his head. "Not necessarily, if Simon Teller offered her enough of an increase to make the move. Nursing's like any other profession—they go where the money is. Did she come with the boy or did she go on the payroll later?"

"I don't know," I admitted. "I'd better find out."

Light, stood up and flexed his shoulders beneath his coat as though relieving stiffness or a burden. "Today's Wednesday. I'll try to check her out at the cop shop tomorrow or Friday. If not, it'll be Monday. I'm going up to San Francisco Friday night, be back Sunday night."

"Carol?" I asked, referring to his problem with the girl who had come out of the desert with him.

"I'm supposed to see her Saturday," he admitted, "but it's mostly company business. They want to discuss this L.A. operation and the possibility of adding a couple more reporters." He shrugged. "I could use the help. A lot going on here in the county."

"Someone's covering for you while you've gone?" I asked. He nodded.

"A kid working on a masters in communications at UCLA. He's not bad, but I think he's more interested in teaching journalism than putting his education to practice." From past conversations, I realized that Sam Light thought everyone in the business should pay his dues by covering police stations and courthouses, and slogging the streets. Maybe he was right.

Several people were standing at a respectable distance from where we'd been sitting. They wanted to talk to Sam, and as he rose, they started to move in.

I walked to the parking lot alone. Sam would be tied up with the others for a time, and I suspected he'd be checking the night man in his office before going home. Since I was already in the Valley, it seemed only logical that I stop off at The Warbonnet and see Sue Tallfeather.

On the drive down the freeway, I remembered something Light had said a week or so ago, when the matter of Carol had come up. "Two things I don't share," had been his wry comment. "My lady and my toothbrush. But first I have to know whether she's still my lady!" He was pretty stoic about the whole thing, but I couldn't help feeling a bit sorry for him.

I had the radio set on an all-news station but turned up the volume when I heard mention of Guns Jensen. There wasn't much. He had reportedly been seen in a bar in Orange County, but by the time the local gendarmes could make the scene, the man was long gone. The rest of the report was background regarding Jensen's jailbreak, which was still being investigated. The cops weren't talking, but it seemed like the press was assuming he had inside help.

A bowling tournament was under way at The Warbonnet, and Sue was running her long, moccasin-shod legs into a bad case of cramps, trying to keep up with the demands of the bowlers and the onlookers. She paused for a moment on her way to the bar, shaking her head at me, with a frown.

"Sorry, Charlie. I'm too busy to take a break. There are supposed to be two of us, but Samantha called in sick."

"See you after work?" I questioned. She shook her head.

"Not tonight. I'm going straight home, soaking in a tub full of bath crystals, then getting as much sleep as I can. I have to do this again tomorrow night!"

I nodded, disappointed, but tried not to let it show. The girl was working her way through college, and I had plenty of respect for that effort. "How about the lake this weekend?"

"I'd like that." She managed to muster a smile, starting to turn away. "Call me!"

The lake was a spot I didn't tell people about. It was about forty miles out of the city and was surrounded by tall evergreens—quiet, peaceful, and beautiful. Maybe it would do something to reduce the coolness I felt developing between Sue and myself. At least, I might learn the reason.

I unlocked my truck and slid into it. I pawed around under the seat until I found the cell phone Jonathon Doom had issued me. I dialed his number and he picked up almost immediately.

"Jonathon Doom here," the same greeting he'd always used in his television show.

"Hello, 'Jonathon Doom here,' " I answered. "It's Cougar. I talked with Sam Light. He'll play along on the Teller thing, but maybe you'd best start thinking about what you're going to give him in exchange. He's going to check the nurse for a police record. Knowing him, I'm sure he'll go deeper than that."

"I don't have anything else to give him at the moment," Doom replied.

"Think 'Scarlet Canary' when we get down to that one," I suggested.

"We don't even know what the Scarlet Canary's all about," Doom protested. "Could be nothing."

I told him I was going home to bed. He agreed it was a good idea.

Chapter Nine

Georgie Huerta woke me the next morning a little after six-thirty. For a moment, I didn't recognize his voice, nor could I get a handle on what he was trying to say. He was extremely excited.

"Whoa! Whoa! Slow down there!" I barked into the mouthpiece.

"It's Georgie, Charlie," the voice stated, sounding somewhat chastised.

"Now I can hear you. Are you okay?"

"I'm fine," he declared, his voice starting rise, those two words running together.

"Take it easy, Georgie. I just woke up and I'm a little slow this early in the morning. How did the stunt go?"

"They found more money. I'm doin' the stunt first

71

thing tomorrow mornin'. Me'n another guy're gonna rig it this afternoon."

"Where're you right now?"

"I'm on the phone downstairs in the lobby."

"In my hotel?"

"Yeah. Wanna buy you breakfast."

"Give me twenty minutes," I told him, and didn't wait for agreement. On my feet, I headed for the shower. With the water running, I managed to shave without benefit of a mirror. I was on my way downstairs with a couple of minutes to spare.

Huerta had taken command of a booth and had two cups of coffee in front of him. He rose, grinning broadly, as I came toward him. I started to greet him, but he grabbed my hand, pumping it up and down, his other hand gripping my shoulder.

I offered a grimace that was meant to express pain and twisted away from the grip. I slid onto the padded bench in front of the nearest cup of coffee and he took the other side, still grinning.

"So tell me," I couldn't suppress a smile at his elation.

"They'll have a video camera out there and tape the stunt, too. They're gonna give me a copy I can show to other producers."

The bulky waitress I suspected had been the first employee when the coffee shop opened thirty some years back was at the table, glancing from one of us to the other. Georgie was still grinning.

"It's too early to be drunk," she observed, "so you must just be happy. What'll you have?"

"Go ahead, Charlie." Huerta urged. "Anything on the menu."

I shook my head, taking care not to look at the waitress. "The house is pretty limited on what it has to offer. I can recommend the steak and eggs. I think I had that once."

"Yeah, once a day and twice on Sunday," the waitress muttered. That brought a chuckle from Huerta. She was still writing on her pad when Huerta nodded.

"I'll have the same," the young Apache told her, still grinning. He made me feel older than I was. There was a feeling of nostalgia with a touch of bitterness as I thought of all the deals that I had messed up, the falls I'd taken, the bones I'd broken trying to make it big in the movie business. I sipped at the coffee, then stared at Huerta, unable to hold back a frown.

"I'm going to give you some advice, Georgie. You made a good thing out of one stunt, but don't let it go to your head. It can be a long while between jobs in this town, so don't turn into a drunken Indian and blow what little money you made."

Huerta looked hurt. "I don't drink, Charlie. You know that."

"Sorry. Figure of speech, I guess." Suddenly, I didn't feel like discussing the movie business and changed the subject. "What do you hear from the Mescalero?"

He offered a shrug. "I don't write much; they don't write much. I was down there a coupla months ago. Saw your sister—she asked how you were. I told her you're sober and doin' fine. I think that made her happy."

I nodded my thanks. The Apaches are not much into women's lib, and my old man had forbidden her to make contact with me. My getting banned from the tribe must really have ruined his relationship with the tribal elders. I'd been told he no longer even admitted I was his son.

"I think most of 'em have forgotten what you did," Huerta said slowly. "We oughta go down t'gether some time an' check things out."

I shook my head. "I was run off the reservation once—I don't need a repeat performance."

Georgie knew me well enough not to argue. It wouldn't have done any good. Besides, that was when the twin platters of T-bone steak, eggs, and toast arrived.

Both of us were wiping up the broken egg yolks with the toast when the waitress came by to refill our coffee cups. She looked at Georgie, then at me, frowning. She jerked her head to indicate him. "He your brother?"

Georgie, lips covering a piece of toast, started to shake his head, but I intervened.

"You could say he's my red brother, yes, but he's not my blood brother." I nodded at him. "This is Georgie Huerta. He is also an Apache."

She glanced from one of us to the other, sloshing the half full coffee pot thoughtfully. "How come you got an American name, and his is Mexican?" she wanted to know.

"Spanish," I corrected her. "The original native language of Mexico is Aztec."

"Okay, Aztec. Why Spanish?" I wondered whether she was going to pour the rest of the coffee in my lap.

"For years after the Apaches were forced onto the reservations, we didn't have names as far as the government was concerned. Everyone was simply given a number. We had our own tribal names, of course, but the Indian agents and the army didn't recognize them. Just the number. When you came in to draw your rations, you had to have the little plaque with your number on it."

"You're lecturing, Cougar," she grumped. "Just answer my question."

"Our people had to spend a lot of time dodging the U.S. cavalry," I told her, sounding like a professional lecturer. I'd made the explanation many times. "Some of the people hid out in Mexico from time to time. When they finally got around to choosing names, some chose names like mine. Some liked Spanish names better."

Georgie saw an opportunity to get into the act. "I think my great-grandfather took the name of a Mexican ranchero he killed. That's the way it was then." He managed to keep a straight face. On the other hand, it might have been true.

The waitress looked to me for verification. I nodded solemnly. As she turned away, I was certain I heard the word "heathens" from somewhere in her immediate vicinity.

Georgie's grin was gone and he was suddenly serious. "I didn't know that about the numbers," he said. "Where'd you hear that?"

"My grandfather. He gave me his number on a little

metal disk just before he died. He taught me a lot. In fact, both he and my father stuffed tradition down my throat 'til I thought I'd choke on it." I thought back to those days of childhood, not wanting to. "I'm glad they made me learn it."

Georgie Huerta didn't like what I was saying and offered a shake of his head. Suddenly, he was back in what had become his real world: Hollywood make-believe. "You got any gags lined up, Charlie?"

I shook my head. "I'm on salary at the moment. I'm running chores for Jonathon Doom."

He cocked his head, frowning at me. "John what?"

"Jonathon Doom. I think he was before your time. I used to do gags for his TV show, when he had one."

"What're you doin' for him?" Georgie was frowning in puzzlement. I had him totally confused.

I shook my head. "I'm not certain myself yet, kid. When I know more I'll try to explain it." I started to slide out of the booth. "Right now, I have to check in with him. Thanks for breakfast."

He raised a hand in thanks and reached for his coffee cup as I passed through the door that led to the hotel lobby. I glanced at the desk clerk and he shook his head.

"No calls. No mail yet, Charlie."

"Thanks." I took the stairs instead of the elevator, wanting to work off breakfast. It was warm in my room and I turned on the overhead fan before I reached for the telephone and dialed Doom's number.

Chapter Ten

"I talked again to Simon Teller about that nurse," Jonathon Doom told me, as he poured me a cup of Kona coffee. I knew he was referring to Helen Boyd. "Among other things, I learned she has Sundays and Mondays off, as well as Wednesday and Friday nights.

"Teller didn't know she had been working at the foundling home while the child was still there. And he said it was his wife who fired a perfectly competent woman and hired Boyd on her own. He wasn't consulted, but didn't think anything about the change at the time."

We stood in front of Doom's picture window looking down upon the street below. I took a sip of the coffee before I offered comment. I'd never heard of Kona coffee until I met Doom. He said it was grown on one of the Hawaiian Islands and cost about fifteen bucks a pound. I'd gotten hooked on it when I'd worked on his series, but I couldn't afford it for my-self.

"Seems to me she doesn't have much time to get in trouble." I had another sip while I waited for his re-action. He was frowning and shook his head.

"Maybe not," Doom agreed, "but I feel certain she's involved in some way."

"That means I have to start trailing her," I stated. We both understood that, of course.

"This is Friday, so she'll be off tonight. Park some-where close to the Teller place and follow her when she leaves the house. See what she does, where she goes. If she meets someone, get a photo if you can. Then Sunday and Monday, you'll—"

I raised a hand to halt him. "Sorry, boss. Sunday's out for me. I have a personal engagement."

I don't know how to describe Doom's expression at my interruption. *Vexed* might fit, if I really knew what the term meant.

"All day?" he asked. I nodded.

"All day and most of the night."

That caused him to raise an eyebrow. "Whoever she is, you could take her along. She might make good cover for you. Tell her you'll teach her how to be a private eye."

"Don't even think it, Jonathon," I ordered. "She's not into this sort of stuff."

"I suppose I could tag along behind her myself on Sunday."

"Boyd's old enough to have seen your series. You'd have to wear a white beard and walk with a cane to keep her from recognizing you," I told him. He brightened at the idea.

"That's not a bad idea. I could start out with the cane and beard, then stash them and change my hat and wear dark glasses. Maybe another change or two." He'd done that sort of thing on several of his shows, but he'd been in control of the stories then. After all, he wrote most of them.

"When she settles in for the night, wherever it is, I could let you know. That way, you could pick her up on Monday morning."

I wasn't enthusiastic, but he was paying me for some personal inconvenience. "That'll work," I agreed, trying not to sound too grudging. Besides, it might not be necessary. If he doddered around her enough with his white beard and cane, she'd probably call the cops. Then it'd be up to me to bail him out on Monday morning. Whatever he did was fine with me. At least Sue and I could still go to the lake, as planned.

"There's one thing, though," my employer stated, choosing his words with a degree of delicacy. "I don't think that truck with the horns is exactly what you need for a tailing job."

I offered a shrug, knowing better than to suggest he lend me the Lexus. "It's what I've got. What about a rental?"

Doom looked out the window, where nothing was moving. Finally his eyes came back to me, and he nodded. "I guess that's the answer." I suspected he had neglected to discuss incidental expenses with Simon Teller.

I called Sue at home to confirm Sunday, but her mother said she was in classes all day. Oddly, I'd never met either of her parents, although I had suggested it several times. Sue had said her father would not like me at all, because I was an Indian. He was a Lakota Sioux, as was her mother, but the old man apparently had higher social goals for his daughter than a man who fell off, and sometimes under, horses for a living. So far, she hadn't had the nerve to tell him about my other job, the process server thing.

I'd been mentioned in the newspapers several months earlier when Sam Light and I had cleared up the killing of a retired stripper, but they'd used my real name, Charlton DeMille Smith, not Charlie Cougar. Sue had not told her father I was both people.

I wasn't sure I would ever meet the man, but what I knew of him disturbed me. From what Sue Tallfeather had told me, her grandfather had taken his wife and son off the Rosebud Sioux reservation in South Dakota and had moved to California to get a defense job during World War II. Her father had grown up in Los Angeles County, and Sue had been born in the Golden State. From what she had told me, it seemed her father had deliberately abandoned his heritage, although for some reason he had refused to change his name to something that sounded less like a reservation redskin. With thousands of Native Americans in the Los Angeles area, he had deliberately set about finding a Sioux maiden to be his bride.

On Jonathon Doom's instructions, I checked half a dozen rental agencies to learn who had the lowest price for what we were after: a medium-sized dark blue sedan with a minimum amount of chrome and flash. He finally approved one that offered a weekend rental at $27.50 a day, plus insurance.

"It's at the airport," I pointed. "I don't want to park my steer horns down there overnight, so I'll have to take a cab. Do I get paid expenses for things like that?"

Doom did not answer my question. Instead, he heaved a sigh and said I could leave my truck in the lot behind his building and he would drive me to the airport rental agency.

"Do you have a credit card?" he asked as we were negotiating the streets to reach the freeway.

"American Express," I told him.

"Put the rental cost on your card and I'll reimburse you," Doom instructed.

It was almost four o'clock by the time I finally parked the blue rental Chevy in the stall next to my truck. I looked around for the Lexus, but it wasn't there.

There was no answer to the bell, so I tried knocking several times. Finally, I dug down in my pocket and found the key he had given me. I opened the door a crack and called several times. All I got for an answer was silence, so I moved in, closed the door and wondered what I should do for the next hour. According to Doom, Helen Boyd didn't get off work on Friday nights until 5:30, so I had a little time to kill.

I tried to read the morning's *Times*, but most of the news seemed to be political. I tossed it aside, then grabbed Doom's telephone, dialing the number for the Stuntmen's Association.

"Charlie Cougar," I announced. "Anyone with a lot of money asking for me?"

"Not with a lot of money, I'd guess," the girl on the other end of the line ventured, "but an outfit called Buffalo Rifle Productions wants to talk with you." She gave me a number in the San Fernando Valley. I'd never heard of them.

As I dialed I knew I was wasting my time. It was almost five o'clock on a Friday. Unless they are in production, most small companies close by four or even earlier, thus creating a slightly longer weekend. I left my number at the Heartbreak Hotel and Doom's number, and said I would check in on Monday morning. I couldn't help wondering what kind of job they had in mind.

I passed a full-length mirror on the way to the door when I caught a glimpse of my reflection. I looked like an Indian in a cowboy suit—hardly the outfit for shadowing someone. I hadn't thought about it, but was surprised that Doom hadn't suggested I wear something less conspicuous.

Behind the seat in my truck was a poplin jacket I kept for rainy days. I pulled it out and slipped it on over the bright Western-cut shirt I was wearing. I deposited my hat, feather and all, on the floor of the vehicle.

I allowed myself about thirty-five minutes to get across town to the Tellers' in the rental car, but it wasn't enough. Friday afternoon in Los Angeles can be a study in gridlock. Everyone is looking forward to the weekend and is in a rush to get somewhere, even if it's just home. It was almost six o'clock when I finally pulled to the curb. I was nearly half a block from the gates to the Teller enclave, hoping Helen Boyd hadn't left.

Exactly twelve minutes later, the wrought iron gates opened and a small yellow sports car slid down the driveway to the street. At the wheel, Helen Boyd braked before turning into the sparse traffic that was headed downtown.

The night was a bust. She drove to a restaurant and had dinner. I was hungry myself and made a point of keeping my face covered with my hand, as the hostess led me to a table in the back of the place. The table she chose for me turned out to be ideal. It was behind a palm and was situated so that I could look through the leaves and see the blonde nurse, but she couldn't see much of me.

I was looking at the menu when a voice behind me growled, "What're you doin' here, Injun?"

It was Lieutenant Brock, who was seated at an adjoining table with a woman. I wondered whether she was a cop, his wife, or both.

"Well," I said, smiling at the pair, but keeping my voice down. "Fancy meeting you here, Lieutenant."

"Nothin' fancy about it, Injun, except the prices. Lenny must be payin' you pretty well."

"Who?" I asked raising an eyebrow.

"Jonathon Doom. Your boss."

"I'm doing okay, I guess." Before he could reply, the waitress presented him with his check. He glared at it instead of me, then growled something to the woman. She nodded and the two of them rose to stride toward the cashier.

I kept my eyes on the menu. For an instant, I wondered whether Brock had also been following Helen Boyd. Then I realized he must have been done with his meal before she had been seated.

I looked up to watch him as he approached the cashier. What was intriguing was that Helen Boyd also was watching him, while trying to hide behind her menu.

Chapter Eleven

T he rest of the evening was pretty uneventful. After dinner, Helen Boyd and I went to a movie. We were separated by about thirty rows, and I was on the opposite side of the theater.

I don't know what the film was about, because I napped through most of it. Covering my eyes with a hand that was propped on the armrest, I'd doze off, then wake up to check whether Helen had outfoxed me and sneaked out. But she was always there.

We were parked in the same lot and I left just before the final credits. I was in my rental bomb when she stalked through the lot and got into her own vehicle. I let her get as far as the street, then followed.

It wasn't much of a chase. I followed her back to the Teller homestead, watched her pass through the gate, then sat on the street, waiting to see whether she came out again. It was well after midnight when I decided that if she was going to make a late night appointment, it was going to be without me

Saturday morning, I met with Jonathon Doom again. He had just finished breakfast, when he let me into his condo. He was wearing a dressing gown with an ascot, and reminded me of the late William Powell.

As an actor, I figured Doom would not like being compared to the late William Powell. I said nothing beyond "good morning," until he had seated me across the coffee table and poured a cup of Kona.

"How'd it go last night?" he wanted to know.

"Nothing to it. We went to dinner, then to a movie. I put her to bed just before midnight, then sat up there watching for an hour."

He cast me one of his quizzical glances that he often used on television when interviewing a witness. "Nothing more than that?"

"Well, there was one interesting moment." I left him in suspense while I sipped a bit of the coffee. "Your friend Brock was at the same restaurant. We had a few words, then they left. But when they walked out, Helen Boyd took one look and covered her face with her menu. It seemed like she wished she was under the table."

"Brock didn't get a look at her?"

I shook my head. "Not that I could see."

"Interesting," he mused, staring out the window, "that she didn't want him to see her. I'll have to watch her closely tomorrow."

That brought us to a subject that had not been discussed. "Incidentally, Jonathon, what are my days off?"

He raised an eyebrow as though I was being impertinent. "Why do you ask?"

"Well, I got a call about some stunt work. I'd like to do it, if I can arrange it with you."

"Hmm . . ." He had forgotten his coffee and was staring out the window again. "Why don't you call and see when they want you to work?" he suggested. "But I'll need you on Sundays and Mondays, and on Wednesday and Friday nights until further notice."

"I'll call them Monday and try to find out," I told him. He shook his head.

"If they're getting ready for a shoot, there's probably someone in their office now. I often worked Saturday mornings—a lot of people in the industry do." There was a formal note in his tone, telling me he was an expert in such matters. It was a good thing I liked the guy.

I found the number for the production company through information and placed my call. The line was busy. It looked like Doom was right. There seemed to be someone there, unless every other stuntman in town was clogging up the phone lines in a try to get the job. I returned to the chair and refilled my coffee cup.

"Well, I did some checking of my own yesterday," Doom informed me, frowning while staring out at the street. "This TV station where they're going to introduce the *Scarlet Canary* show is a little outfit that I used when I was first getting started."

"Used them?"

"It's gotten a bit larger than in my days there," Doom admitted, "but not much. It's a shoestring operation, but it's been good for some of us. It got us exposure."

I didn't know what he was talking about and said so. He drew himself away from the window and settled back in his chair to stare at the ceiling, still frowning.

"The Jonathon Doom series didn't just happen, Charlie. People think it did, but they're wrong. I had written thirteen of those shows, and my agent had farmed them all over town. Nobody was interested. All they wanted was car crashes."

"Even back then?" I asked, thinking of my own career.

"Even back then. I had a little money, though, and I arranged with the station to use its taping crew and stage to do three half-hour segments. The deal was that they would give me their bottom price, if I let them telecast the three on their station.

"I talked to several actors for the part of Jonathon Doom, but they all wanted too much money. I had put up money with the station, and we were getting close to a shooting date. Finally, out of desperation, I decided to play the role myself."

"And you've been playing it ever since," I put in. It was supposed to be a joke, but it earned me another raising of his eyebrow.

"Well, some people got to see how the three shows were made. They may have seen my scripts before, but seeing how it actually played seemed to make a difference. That's how the show made the networks and stayed there all those years."

I never knew any of this and I had a hunch Doom

didn't tell many people. He liked his image just the way it was, not as a one-time unsuccessful writer.

"Ever since then, the station has been sort of a proving ground for new shows," Doom explained. "They're done mostly by independents with a few bucks who want to show others how the project actually looks instead of just pages of a script."

"And that's what the *Scarlet Canary* is? A speculation show someone hopes will be picked up by one of the networks?"

Jonathon Doom nodded. "I still have some connections, a few acquaintances down at the studio. I went down yesterday afternoon and talked to a couple of them. The *Scarlet Canary* is being produced by someone named Bob Buchman."

Doom paused long enough to cast me an inquiring glance. I shook my head. "Never heard of him."

"Neither have I," Doom answered, "but he may be relatively unimportant. The station folks think the money is being put up by Linda Jensen."

"Where would she get it?" Doom shook his head, looking out the window once more.

"From Guns Jensen. Apparently, they had some sort of prenuptial agreement that, if he got sent to prison, she became the trustee of his money. If he dies, she inherits the loot he has stuffed in banks in Switzerland, the Bahamas or wherever!"

I sat up straight, staring at him, recalling the rattled female who had come storming through the door. "Maybe someone really is trying to kill her," I suggested. "Somebody who's upset about all that money. Maybe that's why Guns broke jail."

"Some of his old mob may feel unhappy about all that loot going into television pilots. I'm sure some of them feel they deserve the loot more than a woman who was married to Guns for only a few months."

"So what do we do?" After all, the woman was not a client. On the other hand, I had worked on enough *Trouble, Incorporated* shows to know that the Jonathon Doom one saw up on the screen was more interested in solving cases and helping others than in money.

He shook his head and turned to look at me with a smile. "Maybe we ought to ask her!"

"Wasn't her show supposed to be on last night?" I asked. "Did you see it?"

Doom shook his head. "I saw a couple of minutes of the tape they were running at the studio, but that was all. I was busy talking to my contacts."

"Then we know they tape the thing first and play it on Friday nights. They're doing three of them as pilots?"

"So I was led to believe."

"We'd better find out when they're rehearsing and taping the next show," I suggested. "We ought to be able to catch her then."

"I'll find out when they have the stage reserved for rehearsal," Doom promised. "I don't want to talk to her when she's taping—too much pressure."

"Did any of your contacts happen to know where the Scarlet Canary has her cage?" I asked. Doom shook his head, not impressed with my effort at humor.

"They don't know. This guy, Buchman, handles

everything, including Linda. She even shows up in the mask. Apparently even the people on the show don't know who's hiding behind it!"

I nodded. I had seen a little item in the paper a week or so back about a mystery woman who wore a mask to rehearsals. I'd thought it was press agent hype.

"When's your friend Light due back in town?" Doom wanted to know.

"Tomorrow night, I think. He didn't have a chance to do much digging on Helen Boyd or we would have heard before he left."

"Anything else?" I asked, as I stood up.

"Not that I can think of," he said slowly, then glanced at me. "Where'll you be tomorrow?"

I smiled at him, shaking my head. "I told you, personal business. I'll be so far back in the mountains that not even a cell phone can find me."

He heaved a sigh, as he got to his feet, straightening the skirt of his brocade dressing gown. "Ah, well," he declared, "I'll just have to make the best of it with that Boyd woman."

"You got your white wig and cane ready?" I wanted to know.

His answer was a snort and a finger pointing to the door. I took the opportunity to escape before he dreamed up some Saturday morning chores that he would insist only an Apache warrior could handle.

I drove back to the Heartbreak Hotel, parked in my marked spot, and made a shortcut through the back door of the bar. There was a message from the production company at the registration desk. Apparently they had gotten my number from the Stuntmen's Association. In my room, I stuck my hat in the closet and pulled off my boots. I then dialed the number I'd been given, and a young male voice answered.

"Oh, yeah, Charlie. This is Billy Specht. We worked together a couple of years ago."

"Yeah. It's been a while," I didn't remember him at all. "Understand you have some sort of gag you want handled. First, when does shooting begin?"

"Right. Call is for Wednesday night; it's a night shoot. You have to drop off a second-story balcony, hit the ground, and come up running. It's good for three hundred."

"For that kind of money, I only give you one take," I told him. "And I rig my own gag."

Specht hesitated for a moment. "That sounds okay to me," he agreed. "When do you want to rig it?"

"Where's it going to be?"

"We're doing it in a new real estate subdivision," he explained. "Using one of the model homes. It's a trade-out publicity deal of some kind." He named the location and I wrote it down.

"I'll bring what I think I need. I'll be there about three-thirty. I want to get it rigged and ready before dark." A thought struck me. "Why'd you call me, though?"

"Well, the guy you're doing is supposed to be Japanese. We figured you'd pass!"

"Why didn't you hire a Japanese?" I wanted to know. That brought a laugh.

"Where've been, Charlie? They don't do stunts, they buy the studios! See you Wednesday."

I sat back and thought. I'd need a panel of half-inch

plywood, a couple of two-by-fours, knee and shoulder pads, and ankle braces. I wanted to rig the stunt myself, because the one time I had left it to a studio prop man, he had used quarter-inch plywood, held up at each end by the pieces of timber. When I came off a two-story balcony and hit the thin plywood, it buckled as it should, but it buckled right down to the ground, not acting as a spring. I thought I'd broken both ankles!

There's a popular question among working stuntmen, and I was beginning to ask it of myself each time one of these jobs came up: How many more times can you bust your tail?

Chapter Twelve

The Bible says that God created earth in six days, and on the seventh day he rested. However, the calendar on the back of my closet door says Sunday is the first day of the week, and I tend to do my planning on that schedule.

The calendar and Sunday tie in with one of my personal superstitions as well. In my experience, if Sunday turns out to be a dog of a day, the rest of the week isn't going to be much better. In most instances, it only gets worse.

When I rolled out of bed early Sunday morning, the sun was throwing a rectangle of brilliance on my worn carpet. This was the day Sue Tallfeather and I were supposed to go up into the San Bernardino Mountains to loll around the little lake I had found up there. It was hidden deep in the evergreen forest, a bowl between the mountains. It probably covered no more than five or six acres, but it was beautiful. More importantly, it was a quiet spot that allowed me to get back in touch with myself.

It would be smoggy in the San Fernando Valley, and I considered that a plus of sorts. Sue would be happy to get up on the mountain and breathe fresh air. The air protection people keep saying our smog problem is improving, but they're like TV weather forecasters. They never look out a window to see what's really happening.

I had called Sue at The Warbonnet the night before to learn that she would be going to church Sunday morning, but should be home shortly after eleven. I told her that was fine. I'd go to the AA meeting down the street and pick her up about 11:30.

"Why don't you come out here and go to church with me?" she asked. "It wouldn't hurt you, Charlie."

"My meeting's in a church basement," I told her. "I think I need to be there."

There was a moment of silence before Sue offered a little laugh. "Maybe you do need the meeting, Charlie. After all, you're seeing a girl who works in a bar!" Before I could come up with an answer, she had added, "See you after church, love," and hung up. I had gone to sleep pondering the fact that this had been the only time in our relationship that the word love had been mentioned.

I dug a lightweight maroon windbreaker out of my closet and slipped it on, then donned my hat with the eagle feather and checked my appearance in the mirror.

The meeting was led by a working writer who developed situation comedies for television. He was introduced only as Hank, although most of us knew his full name.

"Just once," he announced, "I decided I'd drink as much as I wanted for as long as I wanted. It took ninety-three days and seven thousand dollars. I awoke in a motel room one morning a few minutes after six. There was a saloon open a block away, but as I lay there staring at the ceiling, I decided drinking wasn't fun anymore.

"Shaking like a leaf, I found an AA meeting that morning. That was six years ago last July, and I've never had the urge since."

There were some rustlings among the members, vague movements from those who either didn't believe his story in entirety or disapproved of his approach. He held up his hand to silence them.

"Mind you, I do not recommend my method to anyone else," he announced. "Everyone has to find his own way."

At 10:30 or so, I attacked the Sunday morning traffic, which was reasonably light. A lot of people flee the city Friday evening for the mountains, beaches, or the desert. Later, when they try to get home, it's usually bumper to bumper all the way to the Mexican border!

When I drew up in front of the Tallfeather residence, I noted that Sue's little Toyota was parked at the curb. The garage door was open, but there was no car within. I wondered where her parents might be.

Maybe still at church. Sooner or later, we were going to have to meet.

I started up the sidewalk toward the door of the house, as the garage door dropped slowly with an electric hum. Sue came bouncing out of the house, pulling the front door shut. She came toward me, a vision in a light blouse and designer jeans. When working, she always wore her long hair in pigtails, but today her hair was down, reaching almost to her waist. I caught her on the sidewalk and put an arm around her, kissing her lightly on the lips. At the same time, I was running the fingers of one hand through the silk-like black tresses. Finally I pulled away and looked at her. She was smiling.

"That was fun," I announced. "Let's do it again!"

She glanced about to see how many of her neighbors were watching, then shook her head with a grin. "Later. Let's get out of this smog." She wore little makeup except for lipstick, and looked like what she was: a college student going on a Sunday afternoon outing.

An hour later, the smog was still with us, lying heavier in the depressions and other low areas, but it began to thin as we moved into the mountains.

At one point, conversation hit a temporary lull. We had been talking about her classes and my effort to give Georgie Huerta a hand. Sue then cast me an odd look.

"Charlie, I have a question." Gazing between the steer horns up front, I kept my eyes on the road.

"Ask," I instructed.

"How is it that you talk the way you do?"

"Huh?" That was enough to cause me to turn and look at her. She wore an amused smile.

"Most of the Indians I've known speak English like they have a mouth full of marbles. And they don't always use the correct words for what they are trying to say. I know the reservation system isn't all that great, but you speak better English than I do!" Her smile had turned to a slight frown, almost as though she was angry at my diction. I had to laugh.

"How come?" she demanded. "Quit laughing!" She punched me on the shoulder with a loose fist.

"Well, I think I told you I did a couple of years at state college on a rodeo scholarship. Then, when I got run off the reservation and got sober, I had to accept the fact that I was stuck in a white man's world." I picked the words carefully, speaking slowly, still watching the road. "A couple of winters, when I wasn't rodeoing, I enrolled at the University of New Mexico in Albuquerque for courses in English and Speech."

She shook her head. "You never let on that you're college-educated."

That earned her another glance. "I'm not. That's all I took—English and Speech."

She thought about it for a moment before asking, "Has that helped you compete in a Caucasian world?"

I offered a shrug. "I don't know, Sue. In fact, I don't know how we're supposed to define the white man's world. Look around you. There're all kinds. White, red, black, yellow, and a lot of in-betweens. Some Indians come off the reservation and seem to do okay. Others come to the cities to look for a better life, but end up on food stamps. Exactly where I stand in all this is something I'm still trying to figure out."

The road narrowed and I slowed down, looking for the turn-off I'd discovered a year earlier. We passed a road that had been cut recently by a bulldozer, and Sue pointed at it. "That's it, Charlie!"

No." I looked back at the area in my rearview mirror. "We're looking for that trail. Remember?"

"That's it," Sue insisted. Her head was turned and she was looking out the rear window. "It's not just a trail anymore."

I found a spot wide enough to turn around. We drove back along the blacktop until Sue pointed to what was now a single-lane dirt road cut through the evergreen timber. I stopped the truck and surveyed the area to identify several familiar landmarks. Sue was right.

I must've been scowling, and Sue had a puzzled, unhappy expression as we followed the new roadway. Originally, it had taken a degree of driving skill to keep from hooking the steer horns on overhanging greenery. Now the path was clear. What remained was a tunnel-like route through the forest, following a crude road of red dirt and rock.

After a mile or so, we could see the lake and I began to feel less apprehensive. But that changed in a hurry. First, I noted several soft drink cans along the roadway. Then we came to an area where all the trees had been downed and the stumps pulled. Four ramshackle cars were parked in what was meant to be a parking lot. Toward the lake, we could hear rough adult voices and the high-pitched laughter of children. I couldn't make out what was being said, but I didn't care.

I looked at Sue and she looked at me. I don't know what my own expression was, but her face held sadness. She shook her head, her tone echoing her feelings. "Nothing ever stays the same, Charlie. I wish it did."

"Don't sweat it, honey. I'll find us another lake— one nobody knows about." I hoped it was a promise I could keep. Then I breathed a sigh of defeat when I saw the enameled sign propped up against a tree. It had yet to be erected, but it indicated this was a new government park development for the benefit of the people of California.

It's Sunday, I was thinking. If my personal history and observations were an indication, I had a tough, unpleasant week ahead.

Chapter Thirteen

W e did not have a hurricane or an earthquake on Sunday, but the day became successively less enjoyable. Disturbed and angry that the state of California was turning our secret lake into another public park, I drove on up the mountain until I found a bench that should have overlooked the San Gabriel Valley and even part of East Los Angeles. Due, I guess, to all of the Sunday drivers, the smog below had thickened. We could hardly make out the lights in the near distance.

Sitting in my truck, Sue and I munched the sandwiches I'd brought and washed them down with ginger ale, but it wasn't what it should have been. During those few Sundays Sue and I had spent lolling around the lake, a couple of fishing lines in the water, the scene had almost seemed like home.

Sitting there in the truck that particular evening,

looking out across that the brown cloud that obscured humanity, I told her how I felt. Lying there, flanking the still waters with her beside me, had taken me back to my days as a kid. Back then, I'd had my own horse and the run of the reservation, exploring and investigating as I learned many of nature's secrets. But having her there with me added a new dimension. It was almost like we were family.

When I finished telling her, she turned in her seat and kissed me. It was a lingering kiss, and I think we both felt sentimental by the time she pulled away and said softly, "Let's go home, Charlie."

When we pulled up before her parents' bungalow, there was a big Buick in the driveway. Sue muttered something I was sure was Sioux. It certainly wasn't English, and it sounded as close to a curse as is heard in any of the Indian languages.

"Who is it?" I asked, nodding to the parked car.

"It's my folks. I didn't expect them back until morning!"

"Oh?" She'd suggested we go home and she certainly hadn't meant the Heartbreak Hotel. Now this. She turned to give me an apologetic look.

"They went to Santa Barbara for the weekend," she explained. 'To see old friends. I was going to invite you in, but I don't think this is a good time."

I was scowling, I suppose, when I looked into her eyes. "Look, I'm not afraid of your old man," I told her. "We have to meet sooner or later."

"Not now, Charlie. Yes, you have to meet, but not now. They'll be tired and cranky after fighting Sunday traffic."

I nodded gloomy understanding, and she bent across the seat to kiss me again. It helped some. Then she opened the door. "I have to go, Charlie. Call me tomorrow."

She slammed the door without waiting for my reply and ran up the sidewalk to the house. I watched until she closed the door behind her, then started the engine to pull away. Yep, it was going to be a lousy week!

Back at the hotel, I had a note in my box saying Doom had called. He wanted me to contact him on his cell phone. I glanced at my watch. It was a couple of minutes before eight.

I dialed and Doom picked up almost immediately. "That you, Charlie?"

"It's me," I told him. "What's happening?" I could hear disco music in the background.

"I'm in some disco place," he verified, "trying to keep track of our girl. She's led me on a chase today. We went through half of the department stores in Beverly Hills without buying anything. Had I not been watching closely, I would have thought she was shoplifting!"

"What's with the disco?" I wanted to know. "Are you going to dance with your white wig and cane?"

"I put those away some hours ago. I am now a gentleman out on the town with a beard and horn-rimmed glasses." He hesitated, then announced on a grand note, "I'm going to ask her to dance. Maybe I'll learn something."

"Then what?" I wanted to know.

"I'm going to stick with her until she goes back to

the Teller house, then I'm going to go back to my condo and get some sleep. If she goes to the Tellers', I want you watching the house no later than seven in the morning. If she goes somewhere else for the night, I'll let you know."

In spite of my frustrations with the lake trip, plus the fact that Sue's parents had voided what could have been a beautiful evening, I managed to sleep through the night until dawn was breaking. There had been no calls, so that meant that Helen Boyd had gone back to the Tellers'.

Before 7 A.M., I was parked half a block from the entrance to the Teller estate. I expected the Beverly Hills police to show up and ask me what I was doing, but it didn't happen. I'd have to ask Jonathon Doom if he'd made some kind of arrangement. If it was the same two cops I'd dealt with in Doom's parking lot, they probably wouldn't remember me. I didn't have the hat, the eagle feather, the boots nor the Western-cut shirt. Instead, I wore jeans, a beige T-shirt, and a pair of high-top tennis shoes.

I could have taken a nap or probably read a paper-back book—a thin one—by the time the blond came through the gates of the estate. As I expected, she turned downhill toward Beverly Hills.

Being Monday morning, traffic was bad, but I managed to keep her in sight until she reached the Santa Monica Freeway. It was almost fender tag a few times, until she cut off and headed toward the ocean.

Helen Boyd knew where she was going, and I followed her through the narrow streets until she came to what appeared to be a cluster of low-rent bungalows, all of them the same general design. She started to pull into a driveway where a battered Japanese truck stood, dripping oil on the concrete. The vehicle looked like a wheeled disaster, with numerous dents and dings filled with unpainted fiberglass. Helen Boyd apparently changed her mind and edged into a parallel parking spot on the street. I drove by and edged to the curb half a block beyond, watching her in my rearview mirror.

She was wearing what could have been a yachting outfit. It consisted of light blue denim jeans and a matching jacket. She didn't have a purse, but her hands were crammed into the pockets of the jacket, so she could have held a small bag there.

As I watched, she strode up the sidewalk to the front door, where she pressed the bell and waited, tapping her foot impatiently. She was at the point of ringing again when the door was opened. I couldn't get a good look through the screen other than to see it was a man, who stepped back to allow her to enter. Then the big white door was slammed shut.

I sat there, watching the house for a few seconds. Doom would want to know who she was meeting and why. There was a clipboard with some lined paper on the seat beside me for notes. My all-purpose windbreaker also was there. There was no excuse.

With a sigh, I got out of the rental car, put on the windbreaker, and grabbed the clipboard. Chances are a neighbor or two would spot me, so I stopped at the house next door to the one she had entered. I knocked at the door and was faced almost immediately by a little old man in a stained sweatshirt and shorts. He squinted at me through milky, questioning eyes.

"What'cha want, son?" he croaked. I offered what I hoped passed as a rueful smile.

"I'm the substitute meter reader, sir. I just need to know where your electric meter is located."

"On the back wall." He waved a hand to indicate the rear of the structure. "Next to the garbage cans." Then he added a helpful note. "Alla th' meters on the block're on the back walls."

I nodded my thanks, saluting him with the clipboard. "Thank you, sir."

"Nobody calls me sir. Name's Bill—Bill Bailey."

"Thanks then, Bill."

He nodded and shut the door. I walked to the back of the house, saw the meter, and pretended to make a notation on my clipboard. Working with concentration, I pretended I didn't see him watching me from the kitchen window. Instead, I walked back to the street, turned toward the adjoining house and skirted the structure, seeking the electric meter. It was where the old man had promised, of course, and I pretended to make notes on the clipboard.

I could hear voices, but they seemed to be coming from the opposite side of the house, and I edged across the rear of the aging structure to turn the corner. The voices were louder and were coming from what I supposed was a back bedroom. I edged up beneath the open window, keeping my head low.

"I don't care what you want, Lex! I'm through with this whole mess!" Helen Boyd's tone was stressed and close to breaking. "I want my share of the money and I'm out of here!"

"Where're you gonna run to, Ruthie?" The man's tone was rough and chiding, as though he knew he had the upper hand. "How long can you play the role?"

"They're already catching on," she snarled at him. "That Indian was at the foundling home, asking questions. He saw my picture! And last night Jonathon Doom was on my trail. He even asked me to dance!"

I had to put my hand over my mouth to keep from laughing aloud, but I wondered who at the Home had tipped her that I'd been there.

"No one can prove nothin'," the man called Lex insisted. "Let's go to the wife a coupla more times, then we'll both head for Mexico."

"Not me. She's tapped out. The only place she can get money now is from Simon Teller, and she won't ask him. It's over!"

"Now you listen t'me, Ruthie!" His voice was harsh with authority, but his next words were an octave higher in tone. "What're you doin' with that gun!"

"I want my share of the money! Now!" The woman's tone was cold, as though she had taken control of her emotions. "Where is it?"

I raised my head then, until I could see over the window ledge. The two were in the center of a shabbily furnished room. The man was probably in his fifties and had a face hardened by life. There was a scar on one cheek, which suggested it had also been a violent life.

"It's right over here," the man said, seeming to surrender. He turned to walk past the woman. She turned, gun still pointed at him, until one of his hands lashed out to grab the barrel and jerk it upward. There was the sound of an exploding cartridge.

The man stepped back, releasing his hold on the gun barrel, as the body fell. He stood looking down at her, his own face expressing his shock and horror. "Helen?" he croaked. "Ruthie?" He started to bend toward her, then straightened abruptly, looking about. After an instant, he disappeared into another room.

I ran around the house and had just reached my rental vehicle when the man came out of the house, a small leather bag in his hand. *Probably the money,* I thought. He hurried to the beat-up car in the driveway and, moments later, backed it into the street. He drove toward me, heading down the hill. I had the engine going and pulled out to make a U-turn, tromping the gas pedal.

The body of the old clunker Lex was driving may have been held together with glue, but there was nothing wrong with the engine! Traffic was light and he was hitting sixty or more on the first block.

Watching the road, I felt around on the seat for the cell phone, but I couldn't find it. Lex dodged around other vehicles and I followed. I was certain that by now he knew I was on his tail. It wasn't until much later that I asked myself why I had taken up the chase. I still don't know.

The hill was a long one, leading in the general direction of the water, but it ended in a cross street at the bottom, where a building was on fire. Through the black chemical smoke, I could see a sign. It was a paint company. Somewhere I could hear sirens, and I moved up on Lex, expecting him to turn down one of the side streets. Instead, he continued straight down the hill, apparently intent on turning onto the street that faced the fire.

As Lex's vehicle neared the bottom of the street, a police car darted into sight in front of the burning paint store, slowed, then moved on. Behind it came the bulk of a fire truck. Lex hit the brakes, surprised, and began to skid, trying to make the turn into the street, while avoiding the fire truck.

That was when his front tire blew, throwing the old clunker off-balance. I managed to slow and was only half-watching as I tried to get to a curb and stop. Lex's truck, out of control, crashed through the front of the burning paint store, disappearing in a veil of dancing flame and smoke.

I managed to pull over to the curb, still a couple of blocks up the hill. The fire truck was pouring water into what had been the building's entrance. It was probably a full minute before the expected explosion told me his Lexus gas tank had blown up.

Sickened, feeling guilty over the two deaths, I sat there for a moment, looking away from the fire. I knew I could not have done anything to prevent either death, but the guilt came from the fact that I didn't even try! Finally, I found the cell phone between the seats and dialed Doom's number. When he answered, I had to gulp a couple of times before I could talk.

"We don't need to worry about Helen Boyd," I told him. "She's dead! So's her accomplice."

Chapter Fourteen

I told Doom what had happened at the San Pedro house, then about following Helen Boyd's killer to the site of his death. There was a long moment of silence before Doom asked, "You're sure the woman is dead?"

"No other way," I insisted. "From what I could see, the bullet went in through her chin and came out the top of her skull."

"You'd better come in, Charlie. Don't stop any-where. We need to talk."

I started the rental car, pausing to look down the hill to where the fire was raging. Two more fire trucks had arrived, and patrol cars were blocking off streets to keep back the curious. Putting the car in gear, I edged out into the traffic lane and went around the block to head back toward the freeway.

I drove back past the house in front of which Helen Boyd's car was parked. For an instant, I considered going in to cover her face in a show of respect for the dead, but Doom had told me to keep moving. There was no one on the street, although it was nearly noon. I took a hard look at Bill Bailey's place, but the front door was closed and there was no visible activity there.

At Doom's place, I parked in the lot and pushed the doorbell. I had to wait a full minute before he let me in, a portable phone held to his ear.

"I don't have all the details, and I don't know how much containment we can do, Simon," he was saying. "First, have your wife get the original nurse back to care for your boy. Then you and your wife get out of town. Leave today. Maybe a business meeting in Brazil?"

There were words from the other end I couldn't hear, but Doom seemed to approve, for he nodded several times while staring at me.

"And tell that maid to give us the run of Helen Boyd's quarters and not to bother us." There was another pause before Doom nodded. "Call me here tomorrow before eight, no matter where you are!"

Looking at me as he clicked off the phone, Doom ordered, "We have to go to the Tellers, but I want to give them a couple of hours to get clear." He heaved a sigh, then was struck by another thought.

"Let's take that rental back to LAX. We don't need it. I'll follow you in the Lexus. We'll go to the Tellers' from there. On the way, you can give me a rundown on what happened."

After the car had been dropped, I got into the Lexus beside Doom, and we headed for the Teller homestead. On the way, I gave him a complete account of my morning. I even told him of my conversation with Bill Bailey, since I figured he might become part of the picture sooner or later.

"But you're under the impression the Boyd woman didn't really want to be a part of this scam?" Doom wanted to know. I wasn't certain I knew how to answer, but I tried.

"It seemed she didn't want to go any farther with it," I told him. "But she did want half the money."

He cast me a frown, stopping for a red light. "What about the money?"

"I think it went with Lex in what looked like a black leather bag. It's probably an expensive pile of ashes by now." I was struck by a new thought. "One other thing. During their argument, he called her Ruthie. Of course, that could be her middle name."

"Or a nickname," Doom agreed, but he didn't sound convinced, repeating, "Ruthie."

"Boss, I'm one of those types that likes lunch. Can we stop somewhere?"

We were headed north on the San Diego Freeway and he pulled off on Sunset Boulevard. There was a restaurant there that was built in a circular fashion. Being on the edge of Bel Air and close to the UCLA campus, I figured it had to be expensive.

"What are we going to do at the Teller place, if they're not there?" I asked between bites. Doom scowled at me for a moment before replying.

"We're going to find out all we can about Helen Boyd. Hopefully, we'll do it before the police arrive!"

I didn't like it. This was the kind of caper J. Doom, Esquire, pulled on a weekly basis for television. It sounded illegal to me, and my feelings must have shown on my face.

"You can back out, if you like," Doom said, still scowling, "but I've been hired to keep the Tellers clear of scandal and tabloid publicity."

I thought about it for a moment, then nodded, unable to hold back a sigh. "I'll play."

At the Tellers', we were admitted by Maria, the maid. She seemed a little less hostile than on our first visit.

"Are the Tellers gone?" Doom asked. The girl nodded.

"They took Brian with them. Señor Teller said to tell you it was not possible to rehire the former nurse." She spoke slowly, picking the semi-strange words with care. "I am to show you to Señorita Boyd's quarters."

It was a nice enough spot. On the third floor, it afforded a view of the city below. There was a bedroom, sitting room, bath, and even a small kitchenette, although the last looked as though it hadn't received much use. I glanced at the maid, who was standing in the doorway, watching us.

"She didn't cook?" I asked. The girl offered a shrug.

"Poco," she replied. "She took meals with me and the cook in the kitchen."

"That'll be all for now, Maria. If we need help, we'll call. Please close the door." She was reluctant to leave, but I guess she understood an order, even if it came from Doom.

"Why're we here, Boss?" I asked, looking around. He was looking into the sitting room—specifically at a small desk in a corner.

"We're looking for anything that will tell us more about Miss Boyd."

Speaking as he crossed the room, Doom was opening and closing drawers. One deep drawer in the bottom had a lock. He tried it, but it wouldn't open. He glanced at me, scowling. "Can you open this without breaking it?"

"I don't know. Let me take a look." It was an old desk, and the lock was antique. I took a folding knife from my pocket and opened the blade. Carefully, I ran the end of the cutting edge between the drawer and the desk frame until it stopped, held there by the lock. Slowly, I began to move the blade back and forth, putting increasing pressure on it. Suddenly there was a snapping sound. I reached down and pulled the drawer open.

"Ah ha!" Doom muttered as he pulled out papers and stacked them on top of the desk. "Just as I expected."

Several manila folders were put in one stack, as well as plastic protectors that held documents. At the bottom of the pile was a thin photo album, which Doom handed to me.

"Look through this, Charlie. Tell me if you see anything interesting."

The album had no more than twenty pages. I began leafing through it, studying each photo, some faded color, others black-and-white. Most of the pictures featured two women. One of them was a younger, thinner Helen Boyd. Her hair had been dark then, and the color shots showed her as a redhead. The other woman in the photo was as tall as Helen and probably weighed about the same. She was a blonde.

I studied the photos one at a time, until I came to a group photo near the back of the collection, which constituted some sort of nursing group. All were in white uniforms posing before an impressive structure I was certain was a hospital. The blond woman was wearing the cap of a registered nurse, as were most of those shown. However, Helen Boyd and several others were bare-headed.

"You'd better take a look at this, Boss," I suggested. Doom shook his head, deep in concentration as he went through the plastic-enveloped documents.

"She's a registered nurse," he muttered. "Graduated from the University of Iowa fifteen years ago. And, according to her birth certificate, she would now be thirty-nine years old."

"In person, she looked older than that," I said, as I glanced into the open drawer to determine whether anything had been missed. In a corner, almost invisible, was a small notebook. I pulled it out and discovered it was an address book. It appeared to be rather old, and most of the names and addresses had been printed with a good deal of care. Some of the addresses were followed by phone numbers; others were not.

Not wanting to disturb Doom's concentration, I slipped the book into my jacket pocket. Closing the photo album, I slid it onto the desk and started to watch over Doom's shoulder. He glanced up to hand me several of the documents he had sorted out.

"Charlie, go find that maid and see if Simon's office has a copier." I understood what he was saying, or more rightly what he was not saying. Going through the belongings of a murdered person before the cops is bad form. To walk away with such belongings would be removing potential evidence. Any good district attorney could send a guy to jail on that charge.

Wandering around the big old house, I finally found my way to the kitchen, where Maria and an elderly black woman were drinking coffee, seated across a small table from each other. They both looked up at me and I nodded to the black woman, who was dressed in white and appeared to be in her sixties.

"I'm Charlie Cougar," I told her. "I work for Mr. Teller. You must be the cook."

The woman gave me a wry smile, showing big white teeth. "That an' sev'ral othah things. You gonna tell me you'ah hungry?"

"No. I need to find Mr. Teller's copier." I held up the parchments and other pieces as an illustration of need. The cook turned to the Mexican girl and spit out something in Spanish. Maria nodded and rose to walk past me. I winked at the older woman and followed. A Spanish-speaking, Southern-drawling cook. She had to be from Texas.

Maria led me to Simon Teller's office, which was paneled in dark wood. I saw the copier and looked it over. I don't know much about electronics, but this one was simple enough.

I ran off two copies of each piece of paper, bunched them all together, and turned off the machine. Maria was standing beside the door, where she had observed the entire operation. Didn't want me to steal the machine, I figured.

"*Muchas gracias*, Maria," I offered, with a nod. Use of two words of my limited knowledge of her language earned me the trace of a smile and a shrug.

"*De nada.*"

Thinking maybe I needed a foreign language or two, I went back to the third floor where Jonathon Doom was waiting. He was still at the desk, staring into space. All of the papers and folders except for the photo album had been returned to the drawer. When I handed him the originals I had copied, he quickly inserted them in their respective protectors, as he spoke.

"You noticed the photo in the back of the album, of course. The one of the nursing staff."

"I did. And I noted that Miss Boyd did not appear to be a registered nurse at that time. I also noticed that she was a redhead in those days."

"I wonder about her friend, the blond," Doom mused, eyes narrowed in the same expression he had used in his old show. For some reason, the thought occurred to me that he might not have been acting as Jonathon Doom. He might very well have simply been doing the real Lenny Squiglemayr! I shook my head. I was getting punchy.

Doom looked at me once more. "It may be time to bring Sam Light into this, if we can get some guarantees from him."

Sam Light was a hard-nosed journalist who liked to

play it straight and tell the whole story. However, except in rare, deserved cases, he generally didn't set out to harm innocent people who might have blundered onto the edge of a nasty situation.

"Sam's not much for guaranteeing anything but the truth," I told him.

Chapter Fifteen

We met with Sam Light in his office downtown. He had started out with one room, but with the success of his syndication service for the outfit in San Francisco, they had given him more space.

He now had a glass-enclosed area the size of a bull-pen that contained only one desk with chair, a computer, several machines that delivered news from various wire services, a muted television set that was tuned to CNN, a wall of file cabinets—and paper stacked everywhere. No one ever gave Sam marks for tidiness, but he insisted it was a common problem in his profession.

Sam was not in when Doom and I arrived, but his secretary said he would be right back. Meantime, she brought us each a cup of coffee. I could see in the outer office there were three other desks besides hers.

Each boasted its own computer terminal and tele-phone. Two of the desks were occupied by young men with severe haircuts and their ties pulled down to half-mast. As a former Marine, Sam Light did not approve of men with long hair.

Doom glanced at the television screen. They were into international news at that point. "I wonder if they'll say anything about the fire?" he mused. It didn't seem logical on CNN; maybe on a local station.

Light interrupted further discourse by coming in and shutting the door. He looked out at the people in the outer room, then pulled the venetian blinds shut.

"I know I have bad news, but this is a little ex-treme," Doom said, frowning at Sam's action. Light turned to him with an ironic grin.

"I have one man out there who can read lips. From what you told me, I don't think we want him a party to what's going to be said." He circled his desk and plopped into his padded chair, eyeing us.

"What's this all about?" he wanted to know.

Doom looked at me, nodding. "Tell him, Charlie."

I began at the beginning, leaving out the Tellers' names. I explained to Sam about the apparent black-mail, the effect upon the wife, and the attitude of the husband. I told him why we had become suspicious of Helen Boyd, how I had followed her to the house in San Pedro, and what had transpired after that. Sam had a pad on the desk in front of him and scrawled hasty notes.

Sam Light cocked his head to offer me a judging look. "You didn't report the killing?"

I shook my head. "I was too busy following the guy

she called Lex, then I had to get back to report to Mr. Doom."

Sam grimaced, then reached for his intercom and called someone in from the other office. A moment later, a curly-haired young man opened the door and looked in. He had pulled up his necktie.

"Come on in, Dave," Light invited. "Call LAPD's Harbor Division and ask if anyone has reported a shooting death today in San Pedro." He looked down at his pad and read off the address. The young man cocked his head, his freckled face taking on a frown.

"If they say they've had no report, tell them we got an anonymous call here. Give them the address, then you get out there as fast as you can. Chances are someone in the PD will call the television stations. I want you there first."

"I'll handle it," the reporter said, head still cocked. "There was a big fire in Pedro they just got out. The AP wire reports that some guy blew a tire and rode full tilt into the fire. His gas tank exploded and blew one of his license plates into the street. They're using that to try to identify him."

"I doubt there's a connection. On your way!"

The door closed abruptly and Light offered a tight nod, still looking in that direction. "Smart kid. He's the one who reads lips."

"If this Lex person lived at his address very long, the cops'll have it from Department of Motor Vehicles real soon. And they're going to find the Boyd woman's body," I put in. "The anonymous call routine is just gilding the lily."

Jonathon Doom had brought a thin briefcase with

him and opened it to draw out copies of Helen Boyd's documents. "It may be that you're in a better position to check these out than we are," he told Light.

Sam Light spread the documents out on his desk, glancing at them. "Born in some place called North English, Iowa," he mused. "Thirty-nine years is a long time, but she may have relatives there." He looked at me.

"Charlie, why don't you get on one of the phones out there? Call information in Iowa. See if you can find a next-of-kin."

I'd done this sort of thing several times. I knew the routine. I asked the secretary to get me the area code for Iowa, and sat down at the desk Dave vacated. She looked over at me a minute later, covering the mouth-piece.

"Iowa has two area codes."

"We want information for a town called North English. We're looking for people named Boyd."

She went back to the telephone and, a moment later, was jotting down the number while I waited. I was thinking about the gag I was supposed to perform on Wednesday, two days hence. The way things were going, I wasn't going to make it.

I'd have to call the production company and try to get them to accept Georgie Huerta as my substitute. It wasn't that tough a stunt, and I could brief him in a few minutes. The secretary turned in her chair and looked at me with a questioning expression.

"I have a Clifford Boyd on the line," she reported. "He seems a trifle deaf, but he wants to talk to you." She pushed a button and my phone rang.

"Hello, Mr. Boyd," I said into the mouthpiece, wondering what the guy looked like. "This is Charlie Cougar with the Citizen News Syndicate in Los Angeles. Can you hear me okay?"

"Lower your tone just a little and talk slowly," the gravel voice somewhere out in Iowa instructed. "Why're you wantin' t'know 'bout Helen Boyd?"

"I'm wondering whether you're related to her," I explained, not wanting to volunteer too much unless he was a relative.

"I'm her father," the voice said. "But why're you callin' after this long?" There was a long moment of hesitation on my part. Something wasn't adding up.

"After this long?" I asked carefully.

"Helen passed away in November 1988. Heart attack, they said."

I wasn't certain I'd heard right. "Passed on? In '88?"

"That's right," the voice said. "Denver, Colorado. She was workin' there. Her ashes're buried right here in th' North English cemetery next t'my wife." There was a long moment before he asked, "What's this all about?"

"It may be a matter of mistaken identity," I told him, not knowing what else to say. "What kind of work was she doing in Denver?"

"She was a nurse in a hospital. Her roommate called t'tell us. My wife was down with pneumonia, so I couldn't leave her. I asked her roommate t'handle th' cremation and send Helen's stuff to us. I sent her the money t'handle it proper."

"What was the roommate's name, sir? Do you happen to remember?"

There was a long moment of silence before he said, "Didn't remember for a minute there. Name was Ruth—Ruth Webberly. She worked at th' hospital, too. They was good friends."

My sign-off was pretty abrupt, and I must have left him wondering what kind of nut the news services hired in California. I looked at the notes I had been scrawling during the conversation and slowly rose from the chair, gliding to the door to Light's office. Inside, I leaned against the door and closed it.

"Helen Boyd was cremated in Denver, then buried in the cemetery in North English, Iowa, in 1988," I announced. Sam Light dropped the copy pencil with which he had been toying, and Jonathon Doom's jaw dropped to his chest.

Chapter Sixteen

"Sharon, call the *Rocky Mountain News* in Denver. See if they have an obit on a Helen Boyd. She died in November '88."

Light was talking to his secretary. "I want to know the day she died and where she was working at the time of death. She was a registered nurse, I think."

Doom was looking at Light with a look of total awe. He shook his head as though finding it difficult to believe what had just transpired.

"Everything's electronic these days," Light muttered. "I figured someone was going to have to start checking out hospitals to learn where she worked."

Doom offered a twisted smile, "It has its dark side, too. With the computer, one can learn things almost instantly most of us don't want known."

"What now?" I asked.

"We can wait a bit," Sam offered. "Shouldn't take long."

"Can I use one of the phones out there?" I asked, gesturing toward the door to the outer office.

A few minutes later, I had Georgie Huerta on the phone. He said he could handle the night jump from the balcony, and thanked me for passing on the gag. He admitted he certainly could use the money. He'd done similar stunts in the past, so I didn't have to explain how. Next, I dialed the production company and said I had what I termed a "legal problem" and wouldn't be able to work Wednesday night. I recommended Georgie and said I had already contacted him. Whoever I talked to wasn't too happy—he accepted my situation, but he wasn't thrilled with it.

Sue Tallfeather answered the phone on the third ring. She had a rigid schedule and devoted most of her time at home to studying and worked three evenings a week. If she had another male interest, she hadn't admitted it.

"I'm glad I caught you," I told her. "I'm sorry about yesterday."

"Ah, yes," she said thoughtfully, faint amusement in her tone, "the man in search of a lake."

"I told you I'd find a new one, and I will," I promised. "But I really called to tell you I don't know how soon I can see you. I'm up to my hips in alligators!"

"You cleaned that one up nicely for me," she added, laughing.

"You're in a happy mood this morning," I noted.

"I should be. I just got home, and I aced the midterm exam I took."

"Great. I'll call you when I can," I told her, "and maybe we'll look for the lake together."

"That could be considered either a deal or a safari," she said, and giggled. "Bye for now."

Sharon—I didn't know her last name—had been on the telephone. She hung up and glanced at me, as she started dialing.

"She was working at the veteran's hospital when she died," she told me. "I'll get the particulars."

"I don't know how much they'll tell you, what with the Privacy Act and all that."

Sharon cast me a glance from behind her glasses, laughing. "Don't make any bets. I'll get it."

"See if they had a woman named Ruth Webberly working there at the same time." I dialed information for the number of the Los Angeles County Medical Association. Sharon was still sweet-talking someone in Denver when I strode back to Sam's office. He was reading the newsprint he had torn off one of the machines, and Jonathon Doom was leafing through an issue of *Editor & Publisher*. Sam laid aside the news story he had been checking and scowled at me, then at the man on the other side of his desk.

"At this point, the smartest thing I could do would be to call Parker Center and tell them what we know," he said. "Let them take it from there." Parker Center is the hub of Los Angeles law enforcement.

Doom closed the magazine and shoved it onto Light's desk. He wore an amused grin as he shook his head. "But you won't. This can be a big story and you want an exclusive."

Sam Light looked tired. I wanted to ask him how things had gone in San Francisco with Carol, but I didn't want to get personal in front of Doom. The newsman shook his head, staring at the telephone.

"Not much I can do here, until I hear from Dave." I gathered he was referring to the redheaded lip reader.

"But let me get a few facts together," he said, reaching for his ever-present yellow legal pad and pencil. "You first, Jonathon."

Light spent the next thirty minutes or so going over the background that had led up to the death of Lex and Helen Boyd. Doom pointed out to him that Simon and Toni Teller were innocent and should not be involved. I could see it infuriated him that Light refused to commit himself.

He was finishing up with me when Sam's secretary marched into the office with a pad in hand. Her face wore a broad grin reflecting accomplishment.

"Helen Boyd was working at the veteran's hospital when she died. It was a heart attack, and happened right in the hospital. She was a registered nurse and was well respected for her knowledge and her manner with patients." Sharon glanced at her notes.

"The woman I talked to in personnel remembered her," she went on. "Apparently, Boyd's roommate took over and made arrangements with a mortuary for cremation and shipping the ashes back to her family. And that's when it gets interesting!"

"The roommate's name was Ruth Webberly and she worked at the hospital, too," I offered. "What was her job at the hospital?"

Sharon cast me a look that said I had spoiled her surprise. Then she glanced again at the notepad. "Ruth Webberly was a nurses' aide. Boyd had been there several years, Webberly less than a year. According to the woman I called, Boyd sort of took Ruth under her wing when she arrived."

"I just talked to the county medical association," I put in, looking at my notes. "A registered staff nurse these days makes somewhere between $18.30 and $23.42 an hour. The top rate requires seven years' experience. A registered nurse can draw more than twenty-five an hour if it's a per diem job, but she draws no vacation pay, no medical coverage or other benefits.

"Then we come to the starting nurse's aide, who makes about eight bucks an hour. The most she's ever likely to makes is about thirteen an hour, and that's with no benefits."

Having said my piece, I glanced at Doom, who was scowling. I wondered whether I was supposed to have passed that info to him so he could present it.

"The simple answer for the Webberly woman taking Helen Boyd's identity would be for the benefits—the money," Sam Light said thoughtfully. "There's a lot of gracious living between twenty-five or thirty bucks an hour as opposed to eight or ten."

The telephone rang and Sharon answered it, then handed it to Light. "It's Dave," she said.

"Talk to me," Light ordered into the mouthpiece. He jotted notes on his pad, with a scowl growing by the second. Finally he heaved a sigh.

"Find out about the license plate that got blown out

the door of that paint store. Get a look at it, if you can, then call me with the numbers. Okay?"

Replacing the phone on his cradle, Light sat back in his chair and looked at Doom and myself. The scowl didn't go away. Sharon stood expectantly at his shoulder and stared at us, too.

"The anonymous tip paid off. The cops got to the house in San Pedro and found the woman's body. They ran the numbers on the car in front of the place and learned it's registered to Helen Boyd. They are assuming the car belonged to the deceased."

"If they check her fingerprints, they'll find it isn't Helen Boyd. It'll be Webberly," Jonathon Doom declared. "And they should check the prints on the barrel of the gun where this Lex person grabbed it. He killed her!"

"There's one other interesting point," Light said. "They found her purse in her car and the address on her driver's license is the same as the house where she got killed. Sounds like she and Lex had an ongoing relationship."

"So she stole Helen Boyd's identity and used it to get jobs as a registered nurse," I suggested. "But I'm not sure how this ties in with blackmail." Doom nodded agreement.

"Chances are, we'll learn she never went to work in another hospital, where someone might get curious about her credentials. Instead, she went to work in private situations or small operations like the foundling home. She probably had enough experience to handle herself in those kinds of situations. Being hired by the Tellers was a real plum for her—she knew something about that foundling home that gave her the ammo to blackmail Toni Teller!"

"That's all very nice," Sam Light agreed, "but where's the proof in all this? How can I write it without proof?"

"You don't need proof for the Teller connection," Jonathon Doom declared heatedly. "Leave them out of it."

Sam Light rose slowly, scowling. "I have to do *something* on this, and it has to be fast," he declared. "Why don't the two of you beat it and let me get to my computer?"

"What about the Tellers?" Doom asked. Light shook his head.

"Let me see if I can make sense of this without dragging in your clients, Jonathon." It was not a promise. He glanced from one of us to the other. "I'll be in touch."

And that was the way it was left for the moment. Sam was turning on his computer when we left, with Sharon leaning over his shoulder. I didn't know how much she knew about the situation in San Francisco, but I had a definite feeling she wanted to be Carol's replacement.

Doom and I were on the sidewalk in front of the building where we paused, watching the mass of humanity that passed by. Most of those we watched were grim-faced and harassed-looking, seeming to be on business they hated.

"So what do we do now?" I wanted to know. "Just wait to hear from Sam?"

"Certainly not," Doom declared. "We have another client to think about."

"Linda Jensen, you mean? She's not a client."

"Not in a contractual sense, perhaps, but she needs help," Doom insisted. "Meet me back at the condo. Meantime, I have to contact Simon Teller. I don't know how he's going to take all this."

I stood there for a moment, as he moved away, almost dancing at the prospect of more good-doing. As for me, I was beginning to feel like I had a part in a continuing soap opera. Problem was, no one would show me the script so I'd know what I was supposed to be doing. There was something strange and unrealistic about the life I was leading.

I was still pondering my uneasiness as I moved down the street toward the parking lot. Considering the neighborhood, it'd be interesting to see whether my steer horns still were attached to my car's hood, and how many hubcaps were missing.

Chapter Seventeen

I didn't want to fight traffic all the way to Beverly Hills if Doom wasn't there, so I called first. I got his answering machine, but didn't leave a message. Instead, I dialed my hotel and asked the desk clerk if there were any messages for me. He read one off from Doom, telling me he was going down to the TV station where the *Scarlet Canary* shows were videotaped. I could join him there. It sounded like a suggestion rather than an ultimatum, but I went to the parking lot and climbed back into my truck.

The television station, as Doom had suggested, was somewhat minor league. It was in the downscale area south of Santa Monica Boulevard, and occupied what appeared to have been a supermarket some years earlier. A new front had been installed, and I noted windows on the second floor, which meant offices had been built up there. Like the windows on the first level, they were protected by wrought iron bars.

Inside, the receptionist glanced up from filing her nails, offering me a tentative smile.

"Can I help you?" She was typical of the breed, in her middle years, but well groomed. I had noted long ago that most studios and other branches of entertainment seem to favor older women for their staffs. The younger ones all want to be stars and take jobs only as temporary measures. They older ladies are more dependable.

"I'm Charlie Cougar. I'm supposed to meet Jonathon Doom here," I told her, hat in my hand. She allowed the smile to broaden, nodding.

"He's with Mr. Sterling right now." She got on the switchboard. "Yes, Mr. Sterling, there's a gentleman named Cougar here for Mr. Doom."

As she hung up the phone, she nodded toward a heavy door near her desk. "Go through there," she instructed. "It's the second office on the left."

The corridor was rather narrow and had a tiled floor. On the right side were several doors with small viewing windows and red lights. These, I guessed, were entrances to the sound stages. Down the corridor, a bent old man was mopping the floor. I expected him to turn at the sound of my heels on the tile, but he just kept working. He wore a battered old hat, his white hair peeking from under it, and a set of coveralls with the name of a maintenance company embroidered across the back.

The office was well furnished and appeared to be permanent, not a weekly or monthly rental. Doom was in a chair across the desk from the man I recognized as Jack Sterling. We'd never met, but I'd seen him around town. He owned the TV license and the studio.

"This is Charlie Cougar, my assistant," Doom stated, as Sterling rose and extended his hand. "We've been discussing security measures for the Scarlet Canary."

Sterling and I shook hands. Then I slid onto the chair beside the one Doom had been occupying. Once seated, Sterling looked at me, offering a frown and a shake of his head.

"Linda had said nothing to me. Nothing to her producer, either. Until this morning, I didn't even know her life had been threatened. Not until the bomb!"

"Bomb?" I'm sure I raised an eyebrow at that mention. Not exactly in keeping with my stoic image.

Sterling nodded. "A rather crude arrangement. The janitor found it in a wastebasket in Linda's dressing room. It was set to go off about the time she would be in makeup for her show."

"What do the cops think?" I asked. He shook his head.

"I didn't call the police. The janitor cut the right wires and I had a studio demolitions man take care of it. A friend who used to work here."

That was enough to make me cast Jonathon Doom a glance, but he ignored me.

"Have you talked to Linda since the bomb was found?" I asked. Sterling shook his head again obviously miffed at having to answer to an underling.

"I called her and told her the taping was being delayed until tomorrow. An emergency I had to take care of. She didn't like it, and the producer liked it even less, until I told him why." He nodded at Doom. "Then Jonathon told me about the truck trying to run her down." He glanced from one of us to the other. "Who's after her?"

"We thought you might have some idea," Doom said smoothly. "We haven't had a chance to talk with her in the past few days." He hesitated for an instant, then stared at Sterling. "What about that million-dollar policy on her voice? Who's the beneficiary?"

"It was her idea," Sterling answered. His expression indicated he thought he was being accused. "I don't know who benefits."

"Was the janitor who found the bomb the one mopping your hallway a few minutes ago?" I wanted to know.

"The same," Sterling stated. "He's new here. The maintenance company sent him over. He'll just be here for a couple of weeks while our regular man is on vacation."

"Maybe we should talk to him," Doom suggested. "How did he recognize the device as a bomb?"

"It was pretty crude. Two quarter-pound blocks of TNT taped together with an electric primer. They were wired to a small alarm clock. Daniel looked it over for a minute, then deactivated it."

"Daniel?" I asked.

"The janitor," was Sterling's identification.

"Maybe we should talk to him," Doom suggested.

"He's out in the hall," I said. "I'll get him."

But the hallway was empty. Janitor, mop, and bucket were gone. I turned and marched back along the hallway to the outer office, where the receptionist was still filing her nails.

"Your janitor. Know where he went?"

"He just left. Said he was done for the day," she heaved a sigh. "He's such a dear. I wish we could keep him instead of the regular."

Back in Sterling's office I told them Daniel had gone, and Doom decided we'd catch him another day.

"It's been a long time since you worked here, Jonathon." Sterling was on his feet. "Let me show you some of the improvements we've made."

We toured the place, which included the second-floor offices around the front of the building. They were separated from the stage by floor-to-ceiling walls. The stage was one big floor, but different sets had been installed in various areas. Carpenters were working on a new one that seemed to be composed of an assortment of roulette-type wheels. A big collie dog lay amid the sawdust, watching the workers. One of them spoke to the animal, and it wagged its tail.

"What's that?" I asked, pointing to the work.

"That's a new game show Bob Buchman is putting together," Sterling explained. "In fact, for the sake of economy, he's one of the carpenters. Let me introduce you."

Buchman was wearing designer jeans and a T-shirt that extolled some past show, but the gloves he wore and the heavy boots suggested he might know his way around a hammer.

Introductions were made all around and Doom offered him a slight frown. "You're the director on the *Scarlet Canary* show, too, aren't you?"

Buchman nodded and the tight curls atop his head shook. His grin seemed authentic. "Gotta keep moving in this business," he declared. "One thing doesn't work, try something else. I'm also the *Canary's* producer."

"How's her show going?" Doom asked. Buchman suddenly became a bit cautious.

"It's doing okay so far, but we've only taped two segments. We were supposed to do another today, but he had to cancel it." He nodded to indicate Sterling, as he said it. Either he didn't know about the bomb found in Linda Jensen's dressing room, or, he wasn't volunteering information to strangers.

"The insurance thing covering the *Scarlet Canary's* voice. How did that come about?" Doom wanted to know.

"Well, it was my idea," Buchman admitted reluctantly, "but I couldn't spare the cash for even one month's premium. The idea was to insure her voice for one month, reap the publicity, then not pay the next premium. Linda paid that first premium herself."

"Any idea who the beneficiary is?"

Buchman offered Doom a troubled shrug. "I suppose she is, it's her voice that's covered."

"How long is that first month's premium effective?"

"About another week." He shook his head. "It didn't get us as much publicity as we thought it would."

The big collie had risen and come over to where we were talking.

"Your dog?" I asked him. He nodded, looking down and petting the animal's silky coat.

"He's my best friend," he said with a soft smile. "He goes everywhere I go."

"Well, I wish you luck with both your shows," Doom said, then glanced at Sterling. "I think we've taken up enough of your time, Jack. Thanks for the tour."

"Can you find your own way out?" Sterling asked. "I have to talk with Bob."

"You haven't changed things that much," Doom declared. "I can find my way."

I followed Doom as we took a route to the back of the stage, found a small door, and opened it. I was surprised to find it led to the parking lot.

"You do know your way around here," I said.

"I should. I spent enough money for stage rental here." There was a grudging note in Doom's tone that I didn't understand.

"It did what you needed it to do," I pointed out. "It got you your pilot tapes and sent you on to the big time."

Doom didn't reply. Instead, he looked over the lot until he spotted the spread of steer horns near the guarded gate.

"What do you intend to do now?" he asked, as he glanced at his watch.

"Unless you have something for me, I thought I'd go see Sue Tallfeather. We haven't had a chance to communicate much what with everything going on."

"Well, it's too late to do much of anything else today." Then he had a new thought. "What's with Sam Light? Is he going to give us a break on the Tellers?"

"That's something I wouldn't push anymore," I suggested. "Sam tends to dig his heels in when he feels pressured." I hesitated, then made a promise. "I'll try to see him early tomorrow and get a reading."

I found Sue at the bowling alley getting ready for her shift. She had on a long-sleeved dress of blue velvet, held at the waist by a beaded Sioux belt. Her moccasins were the same shade of blue and carried the same bead pattern. I suspected The Warbonnet's management paid for some of the costuming. For Sue's benefit, I hoped that was the case. Intricate beadwork is not cheap these days.

"Well," she greeted me with a grin, "it's the lake seeker."

I shook my head. "Not yet, love. Mr. Doom has kept me really busy."

"With things you still can't talk about?"

"I'll be able to tell you all about it soon," I promised, not knowing whether I really was telling the truth.

She joined me in a cup of coffee, then got to her feet. She stood there for a moment, staring down at me. "Charlie, I know how you felt about that lake and what's happened—I feel the same way. But you'll find something for us."

Before I could say anything, she bent and brushed her lips across my mouth. "Keep the faith, Injun."

A few minutes later, back in my truck, I headed for the Heartbreak Hotel. I tuned into an all-news station and half-listened as I negotiated the early evening traffic.

"There is new information regarding the murder investigation in which registered nurse Helen Boyd died. Police say that an anonymous phone call revealed that the late Miss Boyd's last place of employment was a local foundling home, where she was head nurse until she caused a mix-up in prescriptions for the children. At that point, police were called by the management. Miss Boyd resigned her position and disappeared."

We were the ones who had known about that place of employment, and I had a hunch my employer had been the anonymous source. It was a means of keeping heat off the Tellers. The cops must have investigated the tip and learned of the prescription problem and Miss Boyd's departure from the scene.

Mulling this news, I couldn't help wondering, with her lack of formal training, how many other mistakes Boyd had made. And how many might have been fatal.

Chapter Eighteen

"**A**ny idea who tipped the cops to the fact that Helen Boyd—or whoever she really was—worked at that foundling home?" Sam Light asked the question around a bite of the submarine sandwich he was sharing with his secretary. Sitting on the opposite side of Light's desk, facing him, Sharon Cates seemed to be attempting to match him bite for bite. I shook my head.

"Ideas, yes, but nothing I'd want to pass along without proof."

Light cast me an amused glance, then put down his sandwich long enough to scoop up several pages of copy paper and hand them to me.

"Sooner or later, someone's going to check her bank account and maybe even Social Security to learn who her previous employers have been." Sam was as certain as I that Jonathon Doom had passed the word to the cops about the place in Covina, hoping they wouldn't bother to look beyond that period of employment. After all, the woman was dead and they knew who killed her. Case closed. Why look any further, when there were so many other murders that required investigation?

I glanced down at the papers Light had handed me.

WOMAN'S MURDER, FIERY DEATH CONNECTED
By Sam Light
Citizen News Service

Harbor Division officers of the Los Angeles Police Department feel certain a woman found dead in a low-rent San Pedro home was slain by a man who died a fiery death, when the vehicle he was driving went out of control and plunged into a burning paint store near the San Pedro waterfront.

The dead woman has been identified tentatively as Helen K. Boyd, a registered nurse. The man who died in the fire is thought to be Lex Barton, described by an anonymous police source as "a small-time grifter who had served time for fraud and attempted blackmail." Barton had been renting the home where the woman's body was found. Neighbors told investigators he had lived there for several years, and that a woman fitting Miss Boyd's description was a frequent visitor, sometimes spending the night.

Investigators also learned that Miss Boyd was

*an employee of a foundling home in Covina until
approximately six months ago. The handgun with
which she was slain is unregistered. Fingerprints
found on the grip and the gun barrel are being
checked with the FBI files in Washington, D.C.*

*Bill Bailey, residing next door to the death
scene, reported hearing the shot and seeing the
man identified as Barton run out of the house, get
into his truck and speed away.*

*A burned but legible license plate blown into
the street when the truck exploded in the fire was
used to determine that Barton was the registered
owner of the vehicle. Harbor Division police,
aided by homicide detectives from Parker Center,
are continuing the investigation.*

*David J. Worth and Sharon Cates contributed
to this report.*

"It'll be in the morning papers," Light said, when
he saw that I was finished reading.

I folded the sheets carrying his story. "Can I take
this along? Incidentally, I think Doom owes you one.
You don't seem hung up on the Public's Right to
Know."

Sam leaned back in his chair and shook his head.
"The tabloids use the Public's Right to Know as an
excuse to ruin people's lives. Tell Doom not to get
excited. Like someone said once, 'It's not over 'til it's
over'! When they find out the prints on that gun be-
long to someone named Ruth Webberly, all hell may
break loose!"

I nodded as I pushed my way up out of the chair.

"There's that," I agreed, "but at least Toni Teller's being protected from all this."

"So far. It's not likely that what appears to be a lovers' murder/suicide will make the papers as far away as Rio."

I was amazed. "How'd you know where they went?"

Sam offered me a wink. "It's in the business section. Simon Teller's checking out business opportunities down there. It says he took his wife and son with him."

Doom, again? I wondered. "I'd better get moving."

I rose and reached the door in time to open it for Sharon.

"Congratulations," I said. "I see you're now a reporter."

"Not exactly. I only contributed, but it's a step up from being strictly a secretary. Maybe you and Doom should have been credited, too."

"That's not the way it works." I nodded to the door to Light's office. The blinds were closed, so I couldn't see him. "Be kind to him. He needs it right now."

"I know." She looked toward the closed blinds, too. "And I'm trying." Her expression suddenly showed concern I hadn't seen before. "But he's the kind of guy who hides inside himself. He doesn't let the hurt get out. It might be better if he did."

"Bad image for a tough reporter," I reminded her, changing the subject. "You ought to get a raise for your work on this."

That brought a smile and a nod toward Light's

closed door. "I've made that suggestion. Maybe he'd listen to you!"

Still clutching the printed story on the San Pedro events, I stepped back to Sam's door, opened it a crack and called, "Give this girl a raise, Sam!"

I shut the door quickly and headed for the elevators. Sharon was giggling somewhere behind me. I liked her. I thought Sam should, too.

Back on the street, I headed for the parking lot to ransom my truck. Along the way, I absorbed the various smells, ranging from kimchee and garlic to hot Mexican peppers. Mixed in were the odors of Chinese, Mexican and Italian cooking countered by greasy hamburgers and hot dogs. Someone once called Honolulu the Melting Pot of the world, but that person must never have been to Los Angeles. They were all there: the whites, the blacks, the reds, the browns, the yellows, and all sorts of hues in between. And most of them looked as though they had the weight of the world on their shoulders.

The area depressed me beyond belief. More than once I'd wondered what a nice, sober Apache boy was doing in such a place, when there were all those trees, mountains and rivers where I came from. Once in a while, I had to admit to myself I was homesick for the Mescalero.

I had meant to ask Sam if there was any late news on the whereabouts of Guns Jensen, but it had gotten pushed into the back corner of my mind.

Chapter Nineteen

Bob Buchman was an entirely different man in a suit and tie. He looked like a television producer rather than the carpenter he had been the day before. The friendliness during our earlier visit had been replaced by an air of suspicion that verged on open hostility.

"This is our taping day. It's already been postponed once," he announced. "This is no time to be upsetting the Scarlet Canary."

"We don't intend to upset her," Doom offered in a soothing tone. "We only want to reassure her that we're here to help."

Buchman considered that for a moment, still scowling. "How much do you know?"

"We know she thinks someone is trying to kill her, and it would seem her fear has a degree of validity," Doom stated. "We also know her real identity. So do the cops, incidentally. It's not like you're protecting any big secret."

While Doom was doing the talking, I was looking around the stage. Buchman's dog lay on a folded blanket at the edge of the big room.

At the back of the stage, where the set for the Scarlet Canary show was situated, the white-haired janitor was sweeping the floor. This time, I had the opportunity to get a good look at him. His hair was totally white and rather long. He also had bushy white eyebrows and a scrubby beard that was probably a week or two old. He was round-shouldered and moved as though getting one foot ahead of the other was painful, but there was something about the old man that just didn't fit. I wasn't able to identify the quality or lack of it, but the impression didn't go away as I turned back to the others.

Buchman had adopted a baleful look as he listened to Doom. He shook his head with a grimace of disgust. "This whole thing has been a mess from the day Linda showed up here and was willing to pay to do these shows." He glanced past Doom's shoulder and nodded to the set for the game show he was developing. It appeared that the carpentry work was complete, and several protective tarps had been laid out along with gallon paint cans for the next phase.

"If I hadn't needed the money to get my own project going, I wouldn't have signed up to produce and direct her show." He looked around and offered a hopeless shrug. "She's supposed to be here now. The musicians are due here in twenty minutes, and I haven't even had a chance to talk to her about the script. We had to revise it after rehearsal the other day."

"You needed her paychecks to finance your own project?" Doom asked. He was frowning. "That doesn't sound like Jack Sterling. He used to be open to all sorts of piece-of-the-show actions. He was willing to gamble a bit; he did with me."

Buchman nodded. "True, but that was way back when. It's cash up front these days." He waved a hand to indicate the entire stage. "And as you can see, production's not exactly efficient around here. There are one-stage studios all over town these days that are cheaper."

"The Scarlet Canary paid cash up front, too?"

"As far as I know, she did," Buchman said, then added, "But now I'm talking about things that're none of my business."

"Is Sterling here?" Doom asked.

"He was back here a little while ago, playing with my dog. I think he went to his office."

I glanced once more at the dog, noting that it was sleeping. Tough life. I followed Doom and Buchman to the corridor door that led to the series of offices and dressing rooms. I glanced back, expecting the dog to follow its master. It had not moved, and there was no sign of the white-haired janitor.

We had to pass the row of four dressing rooms before reaching the executive area. The janitor was coming out of the room with a big silver star and a decal of a bright red canary on the door. He was carrying a black plastic trash bag that seemed to be about half full.

"Is the Canary here yet?" Buchman asked. The janitor looked at him for an instant, almost sullen. Then he dropped his head, as if to inspect the floor.

"She just came in," he muttered. "Chased me out. Said she had to change."

"I have to talk to her," Buchman told Doom. "You can find your way to Sterling's office, can't you?"

Doom offered an amused smile. "I always have."

Buchman was tapping on Linda Jensen's door as the janitor was entering the adjoining dressing room, black trash bag in hand. I had a chance to check his name tag: Daniel Denny. Unusual. Almost like a show biz name. I wondered if his friends called him Danny Denny. Probably not. Actually, he looked old and lonely, as though he didn't have friends.

There was no one in Sterling's office, so we proceeded to the receptionist's post.

"Any idea where we can find Jack Sterling?" Doom asked.

The receptionist laid aside her emery board and reached for the telephone. "Go on into his office. I'll page him."

With a sigh, Doom retraced his steps and led me into Sterling's office, while the sound of the public address system informed Sterling that we were waiting.

"I didn't know you were coming in, Jonathon," Sterling announced, as he bustled into the office. He indicated the two chairs across from his desk. "Please. Have a seat, both of you."

He rounded the desk to settle into his own padded

model, leaning back to eye us. "What can I do for you today?"

Doom was frowning again, and shook his head as though confused. "I thought I knew this operation pretty well, Jack, but maybe I don't. You used to gamble on a lot of shows, letting people use your facilities for a piece of the action. I understand that's all changed."

Sterling offered Doom a quizzical smile. "You've been talking to Buchman," he declared.

"That's right. We have."

"Bob's pretty upset with me right now. Out of the past four shows he's developed, not one has sold to a sponsor. In fact, I put them on the air with the idea that my station could sell sponsor time locally, but we didn't even recover costs."

"Buchman's a loser?" Doom wanted to know.

"He's still thinking ten years ago," Sterling explained. "He tried a couple of teen shows without knowing the first thing about today's high school kids. And there were others that were just too far behind the times. Credit has to stop somewhere."

"What about the Scarlet Canary?" Doom wanted to know. Sterling shook his head.

"She's a nice young lady," he announced, "but nothing special. She came in and talked to me about doing this mystery singer thing. There was something like it on radio way back when, and it went over big. But in those days, there was only a voice and people had to imagine what the singer looked like. I don't know whether viewers today will be intrigued by a girl they figure may be so ugly she has to hide her face."

"But you were willing to gamble on her?"

Sterling shook his head. "Not really. She came in with some cash and put up a bond to cover costs."

"How about Buchman? Where'd she latch on to him?" Doom wanted to know. It seemed he was asking questions that didn't have much to do with Guns Jensen and whoever was trying to kill her.

"She'd met him somewhere socially and asked me about him. I figured if he was working, it would be a chance to get some of my money back."

"So you led the little lady down the primrose path," Doom accused. "The old take-the-money-and-run routine."

"Look, Jonathon, she was going to spend her money somewhere. It might as well be here. I have the facilities she needs and, with her insistence, Bob Buchman might even come up with a winning show."

"Well, you've telecast the first two over your station. How did they do?"

It was Sterling's turn to scowl. He shook his head. "It's too early to tell. A couple of nice reviews in the trade journals, but nothing from the local newspapers. We have gotten several hundred fan letters, but they all seem to be from senior citizens who remember the old radio show."

"Advertising?" Doom wanted to know. Again, Sterling shook his head.

"Not enough to pay taping expenses thus far, but it takes time to build a following. You know that."

"The difference perhaps is that I went out and peddled my own show to the networks. Is she qualified to do that?"

Another shake of the head. "I don't think she's even trying. We're getting ready to tape the third segment. I'll telecast it next week. Maybe then, she'll take all three tapes and try to sell it."

"Nothing has changed in this business," Doom muttered, glancing at me. "The blind are still leading the blind."

"It's changing faster than anyone can keep track," Sterling complained. "What with all of these new channels, satellite TV and the Internet, we have competition like you've never seen before. Even the networks are losing viewers and advertisers to the new stuff."

Suddenly there was an anguished cry in the hallway. A moment later, the door was thrown open and Bob Buchman stood there, tie awry, breathing heavily.

"Someone's killed my dog!" he snarled, glancing at each of us as though he suspected all of us.

Sterling was on his feet, staring at the producer. "What do you mean? I was playing with him not thirty minutes ago. He was fine!"

"Now he's dead! What did you feed him?"

"Nothing but some dog treats." Sterling was on the defensive. He reached into a desk drawer and drew out an imprinted plastic bag. "Nothing but these!"

He tossed the bag at Buchman, who caught it, looked at the package and dropped it on Sterling's desk. "With all the crazy stuff going on around here, why pick on an innocent animal!"

He was close to tears as he whirled and moved toward the door. "I'm calling the police."

"I don't think that'll do much good," Doom put in quietly. It was enough to stop Buchman in the doorway.

"They'll send the nearest squad car to take a report, they'll call animal control, perhaps, and the report will end up with a few hundred others in a basket somewhere."

"What can I do?" Buchman wanted to know. Meantime, I was thinking back to the last sight I'd had of the dog. It had looked as though it was asleep. Earlier, its eyes had been open.

"Let's go take a look," Doom suggested. He rose, nodded at Sterling, and led the way down the corridor. In front of the Scarlet Canary's dressing room, Daniel Denny was tying up the bag of refuse he had collected from the dressing rooms and offices. Two more similar bags lay along the hallway.

Doom led the way, with Buchman between us. I glanced back to note that Jack Sterling had not followed us. Well, it wasn't his dog. Daniel stood back, allowing us to pass, then followed us with his eyes, plainly curious.

"Dead dog," I muttered as I passed him.

The big dog still lay on the folded blanket, eyes closed, as Jonathon Doom knelt beside him. First, he reached into an inside coat pocket for a pair of thin latex gloves such as surgeons and dentists wear. In his old series, he always had carried such gloves. Now, though, I couldn't help wondering whether he was showing professionalism or this was still show biz.

Wearing the gloves, he ran his hand over the animal's body. He looked up at Buchman. "How old is he?"

"A little over three."

Then Doom raised the dead dog's head and pried open its mouth. He bent close, sniffing at the dog's mouth several times. Then he drew back to extend a finger in the dog's mouth. When he withdrew it, on the end of the latex-covered digit was a small gob of an oily black substance that looked something like axle grease. Doom raised the mass close to his nose, sniffing it.

With his free hand, Doom withdrew the handkerchief from his breast pocket and wiped the substance on it. He smelled the mass once more, then folded the square of cloth carefully.

Looking around, I noted that Sterling and Daniel Denny had joined us. All had stood quietly, watching what Doom was doing. Finally, Buchman could contain himself no longer.

"What is it?" he demanded.

Stripping off the gloves, Doom looked up at him. "It's not dog treats."

"Then what is it?" It was Sterling who made the demand this time.

"Curare, I think."

Chapter Twenty

I knew curare was a poison used on the arrowheads of Jivaro Indians in the South American jungles. Looking at the faces of the others, I wondered who else knew. Everyone was stunned, with the exception of Doom, who slowly rose, looking down at the dead dog. Just as slowly, he turned to Buchman.

"I think I know how you feel, Bob. I'll be happy to take care of the remains, if you like."

Buchman shook his head, near tears. "I don't want him incinerated."

It was my turn. "Not even cremated," I promised. "There's a beautiful little pet cemetery down in North Orange County. We could arrange to have him interred there. There could even be a short burial service."

Doom cast me a surprised look, but I knew what I

was talking about. I'd once chased a gravedigger across the grounds, trying to serve him with a summons. That was where I'd tripped over a dog's tombstone and broken my ankle. I never did make service on that one.

"You go ahead with your taping," Doom suggested, "and we'll take care of your friend."

Buchman shook his head. "There isn't going to be a taping. Not today. I can't handle it."

In the background, the members of the band had been watching, holding their instruments. Now they stood around, casting odd glances at each other. They had been hired to do a job that now wasn't going to happen. How was their union going to handle that?

Doom ignored them, putting a hand on Buchman's shoulder. "What was your friend's name, Bob?"

"Mark Anthony." The producer's voice was thick. "I called him Tony."

Doom turned to me. "Charlie, would you wrap Tony in his blanket and get him out to your vehicle?" He looked back to Buchman. "We'll be in touch. Right now, I think the musicians want to talk to you."

Buchman made no move toward the band members as I folded the blanket about the dog. Doom bent to help.

"I'll help you carry him out," he whispered. It was pretty obvious he didn't want Buchman to see that his treasured pet was to be hauled away in an aging truck decorated with steer horns.

Once through the doors and into the parking lot, I led the way, holding one end of the blanket-covered form. Carefully, we lifted the weight over the tailgate and deposited it in the bed of the truck. I turned to Doom.

"You were serious about that pet cemetery?" he asked. I nodded.

"It's there. I'll start down to Orange County now, if it's okay."

Doom shook his head. "Not yet. You have the cell phone?"

"It's in the truck."

"Wait here while I check the receptionist's phone book. I want you to deliver this bundle to a veterinarian I know. I'll get the number and call you."

He turned to stride across the lot, dodging between cars, then disappeared through the side door that opened to the reception area. I was sitting in the truck when the cell phone beeped.

"I'm here," I stated, phone pressed to my ear.

"The vet's name is William O. Hurt," Doom announced, giving me an address in Glendale. "I'll tell him you're coming and why."

Before I could say I'd like to know why, too, I saw Brock, the D.A.'s investigator, heading for the same door through which Doom had entered.

"Uh-oh! You're about to have company!" I announced. "Brock's on his way in!"

"Probably coming to harass Linda Jensen." There was a slight pause. "You get going, Charlie. I'll take care of Brock." As I drove away, I wondered if Brock had seen us loading the dog's body into the truck.

I had no trouble finding the vet's office in downtown Glendale. It was in a little one-story stucco structure tucked between a pair of multi-story buildings.

The squat, flat-roofed building was obviously a hold-over from the 1930s. It looked totally out of place; sort of like a midget at a convention of pro basketball players.

When I glanced at the name on the door and saw how it was spelled, I couldn't help wondering whether the name Hurt harmed his business. Okay, so I have a weird sense of humor.

When I entered, the blanketed body in my arms, I was surprised to find no other customers waiting. For a moment, I was all alone, until a prim young lady brimming with efficiency came through a door behind the reception cubicle.

"Can I help you?" she asked brightly, purposely ignoring my bundle.

"Jonathon Doom sent me. I'm supposed to see Dr. Hurt."

The woman nodded. "He's waiting for you. Come this way, please." She stepped around her desk and I followed her down a short hallway to another door, which opened into what looked like an operating room. There was a steel table bolted down in the center of the floor, with adjustable overhead lamps. I laid the late Mark Anthony on the cold steel surface and straightened up. The girl was standing in the doorway expectantly.

"You don't have to wait, if you don't want to," she said. "Dr. Hurt has talked with Mr. Doom and knows what he wants done. It's going to take some time for the tests, I think."

"I don't know what those instructions are," I told the woman, "but don't dissect that animal. There's probably going to be an open-coffin funeral service at the pet cemetery!"

She didn't know whether or not to believe me, but stood aside as I stepped back into the hallway.

"You'll be able to pick up the remains tomorrow," she called after me. There was a strange note in her tone, and I wondered if she was laughing at my role as a hearse driver for a dead dog.

Back in the truck, I dug out the cell phone and dialed Doom's unit. He answered almost immediately, but the connection was poor.

"I can hardly hear you," he said through the static. "I'm at home in the basement. Give me a few minutes to get upstairs, then call me on that phone."

"No, I'm headed there now—I won't be long," I said, and hung up. Starting the truck, I maneuvered into traffic and made for the freeway. It was early afternoon and traffic shouldn't be worse than usual.

I was wrong. There was a three-car wreck on the mountain road, and it took me well over an hour to finally park behind Doom's condo. Once through the door, I made for his refrigerator, where I found a jug of cold water. He simply stood in the middle of the floor and watched as I downed about a quart of it.

"Feel better?" he asked, when I had set the jug in the sink. I shook my head.

"Not until you tell me what I'm really doing. Is this detecting or are you writing a script?"

"Sit down, Charlie," he soothed. "I'll try to bring you up to date."

I turned back to the cabinet, found a glass and filled it. Then I took one of the chairs next to the window.

Doom sat down on the opposite side of the coffee table.

"Why Dr. Hurt?" I wanted to know.

"He's an old college friend and a good vet," I was informed in a serious tone. "I wanted him to do a minor autopsy to determine how much of that curare got into the dog's stomach, or if more of the poison was introduced by other means of administration."

"I don't know much about curare, except for the old jungle movies where someone would use a blow gun to shoot a dart into some guy and he'd fall dead immediately."

Doom nodded. "Neither do I. That's why I was in the basement. I was looking for some old notes I once made on that particular poison. It was a long time ago, but I seem to recall someone submitted a script for the show with curare as the murder agent. I found something wrong with the idea and turned down the script."

"You still have the script?" I wanted to know.

Doom shook his head. "No. I always returned those we didn't buy, but I also kept memoranda on why they were rejected. I have to find those notes."

"You don't remember what you wrote?"

Doom offered a condescending shake of his head, "Charlie, I may appear to be a bit of a genius in some areas, but I do not have a photographic memory. Hundreds of scripts went through my office, and that was years ago. All I have at this point is a vague recollection."

"Back to the dog. The girl in the office said we could pick it up tomorrow. I guess they'll call you."

"I hope to hear from Bill Hurt this evening. But we still have to make arrangements at your pet cemetery."

"*A* pet cemetery, not mine," I corrected.

"Will you call the place and have them dig a proper grave?" Doom asked. I stared at him.

"Is that any kind of job for a true Apache brave? A tamer of wild horses?" I demanded, offering him my best scowl. Sue Tallfeather knew all about my mis-adventures in the same cemetery with the gravedigger. She brought it up any time she wanted to embarrass me. If I had to complete the arrangements for a dog's funeral and she found out about it, I'd never hear the end of it.

Doom glared at me for a moment. Dissension in the ranks? Then he offered a shrug. "Get me the number," he directed. "I'll make the call."

While he puttered about the kitchen, brewing a pot of Kona coffee, I got the number of the pet cemetery and jotted it down on a pad Doom kept next to the telephone.

"What happened with Lieutenant Brock?" I asked.

"He was there, as he put it, to interview Linda Jensen, but she had already left. She was really upset over Buchman canceling the taping again, and she fired him before she stalked out. Brock tried to get her current address from Jack Sterling, but he wouldn't play. He tried me, too, but I just told him the truth: that I don't know where she's living. He went off in his standard frustrated huff."

"If Miss Scarlet Canary fired Bob Buchman, that means he's out of the picture. He can pick up his own canine corpse from the vet."

Doom shook his head. "I don't think so. I don't want anyone except the two of us to know I took that dog to Doc Hurt. Not yet. I'll make the arrangements and you'll have to take the dog down there for burial." He handed me a cup of coffee.

"Don't you think that's a waste of my talents? I could have Georgie Huerta make delivery of the dog. Once it's delivered, you could notify Buchman and he can take it from there."

"Who's Georgie Huerta?

"A tribesman. Totally trustworthy. And he owes me."

"Let me think about it," Doom murmured, staring out the window at the street.

"Need anything more from me now?" I was back in the easy chair, where I had been watching traffic on the street below.

"Well," he began, choosing his words carefully, "if it's not against the Apache warrior code, I could use some help in the basement, looking for those notes."

It was a good thing I liked his coffee. And considering the alternative, searching a basement beat stumbling over a dog's tombstone—but not by much!

Chapter Twenty-one

It was a few minutes after seven when the phone woke me.

"Is this Charlton DeMille Smith?" a laughing voice asked. I came fully awake in an instant, swinging up to sit on the edge of the bed.

"That depends on who's asking." Then I laughed. It was Sue. "Good morning."

"I woke you up, didn't I?" There still was a chuckle on her tone. "Sorry, but I have come to a decision and you should know about it."

"What decision? Are you going to marry me?"

"You have to ask first."

"Well, you know how it is. We Apaches think things over for a while."

"Next week is spring break at school. A whole week

164

off. If you can get the time, we could go look for that lake together."

I was shocked at this offer. For a moment, I didn't know what to say.

"I know what you're thinking," Sue said. "My father."

"Yeah. I'll probably get a Lakota Sioux war lance through my gizzard when I come to get you."

"Charlie, I am twenty-two years old. I pay rent to stay here. I can do what I like, though he doesn't understand that. I'm still his little girl. He won't even discuss you, and he doesn't want to see you."

"Sounds like a great start for a glorious week," I muttered, a note of gloom in my tone.

"But you do have to satisfy my mother," Sue put in. "She wants to meet you and have your word that you will return me at the end of the week in the same virginal shape as when I left her."

"Maybe we ought to talk about marriage," I suggested.

"Charlie!" There was warning in her tone.

"I can make that promise," I told her finally, "but you'll have to help me keep it."

"That I can do. Any other problems?"

"Not that I can think of. If Jonathon won't give me the time off, I'll quit!"

"Nothing so drastic, I hope. I have to run now. Stop by The Warbonnet tonight, if you can. 'Bye!"

The line went dead and I thought about the trip she had suggested. That meant renting two rooms every night, no matter where we were. My bank account could afford that, of course, but the thought of being so close, yet so far would be difficult.

I got dressed and went down to the coffee shop. As I worked my way through a stack of hotcakes and some bacon, I thought about Sioux tribal customs, about which I knew absolutely nothing.

In the old days on the Apache reservations, a young brave would visit a girl and her family up to five times; then his own family would help him build a separate house. He would move into it, and that night the girl would come and sleep with him, neither of them touching the other. Before dawn, she would go back to her parents' house before they were awake.

The next night, the girl again would come to sleep beside the brave, then cook his breakfast and take his bed out into the sun in the morning. She would watch him eat, but not taste the food. She then went home, having demonstrated her willingness to care for him, cook his food and live with him. His eating what she cooked demonstrated that he was willing to accept her as a wife.

The next part was a bit harder. He had to haggle with her parents on how many horses he was willing to pay for her. Once that was solved, they would go to the Indian Agency offices for a lawful marriage. That was the way my mother and father had been married. The reservation missionaries had since used their influence to develop a somewhat different set of custom rules.

I finally admitted that sleeping in the next room would be a little like the old ways. We certainly wouldn't be touching! I paid for my breakfast, went back to my room, and called Georgie Huerta.

He hadn't been up long, but seemed attentive enough when I told him what I needed. He agreed to pick up the body of the dog and take it to the Orange County pet place. Then I called Jonathon Doom to report that it was under control.

"You'd better call Bob Buchman and tell him what's going on," I told him. "Georgie will pick up Mark Anthony as soon as the vet opens. Buchman can call down to Orange County and make his own arrangements."

"He'll probably miss us as mourners," Doom said thoughtfully, "but it would seem he is no longer part of the problem. I don't think he would poison his own dog."

"What else?" I asked, glancing at my watch. It was a few minutes after eight.

"I tried to reach Jack Sterling, but his girl said he is on the stage getting ready to roll tape."

"For what?" I wanted to know.

"He's replaced Buchman, directing the taping of the third Scarlet Canary show," Doom said. "I think you'd better meet me there as soon as possible."

It had been after midnight when Doom had told me to go get some sleep. He had still been digging through rust-flaked filing cabinets, as I was leaving.

In spite of the fact that he had still been at it when I had gone, he sounded fresh and alert on the phone. Ready to charge any windmill that got in his way!

Doom's Lexus already was in the studio parking lot when I pulled into a spot not far from the side door to the reception area. The same secretary was manning the phones when I entered. She looked up, recognizing me.

"Mr. Doom is on the stage. Go on back, but if the light over the door is red, wait until it goes out to enter."

The light was red, and in front of the door, looking through a small pane of glass, was Daniel Denny. He was wearing the same uniform as the day before, and he had what I assumed was a fresh plastic bag in his hand. He saw me as I approached and offered a wisp of a smile before he turned and shuffled down the hallway. I watched until he opened the door to a rest-room and went in, then turned my attention to the small viewing port.

The band was in place, the Scarlet Canary was standing under a boom microphone, and Jack Sterling was talking to her. There was a flash and I glanced up to see that the light had gone out. Apparently, taping was done for the moment.

I hadn't been able to see Doom through the viewing port, because he was standing just inside the door back against the wall.

"Are they done?" I asked. He nodded, still watching the set where the action had been taking place. Sterling said something to the musicians, who had been wait-ing listlessly. They suddenly began to pick sheet music off the stands and to pack their instruments.

"Can she sing?" I wanted to know.

"Better than I expected," was Doom's reply. Sterling was leading the singer toward us. He nodded, interrupting his conversation with her as they passed through the heavy sound-proofed door and into the hall. Doom was behind them, and I followed.

"I think it went great!" Sterling's voice boomed along the corridor. "We'll have to celebrate."

"Right now, I want to get all this makeup off." Linda Jensen said. She reached up to take off the mask she had been wearing, looking at it with distaste. "Talk to me later."

She entered her dressing room and shut the door. Sterling stared at it for a moment, then turned to stride down the hall to his own office. Doom glanced at me.

"Have you seen Lieutenant Brock around here this morning?" he asked.

"Not so far."

Doom heaved a sigh that didn't tell me anything, then stalked down to the door carrying the star and the decal of the red bird. He knocked, and a muffled voice asked who it was. Doom told her.

"Come in, please," the voice said.

Linda Jensen was standing at her dressing table, smearing cold cream on her face as we entered. She offered a tired smile.

"Sorry to appear this way, but I hate stage makeup. Feels like I have cement all over my face!"

Doom nodded. "I know the feeling, but we all have to put up with such things if we're going to be in the business."

She took a swipe across her face with a soft paper towel, removing some of the grease, then shook her head. "I'm not so sure I want to stay in the business. I thought it'd be fun, but it's more like a squirrel cage." She glanced toward what I took to be a bathroom, raising her voice. "Mr. Denny, are you about done in there?"

"One more minute," came the muffled reply. Linda looked back to Doom.

"When I decided to finance this show, I thought I could control it," the woman complained. "But I guess it's impossible to control sheer madness, and that's what this has become."

"You've been under a lot of strain," Doom offered. "Take a few days and relax. Maybe it'll seem different."

A moment later, the bathroom door opened and Daniel Denny shuffled out, black plastic sack in hand. Closing the door behind him, he didn't seem surprised at finding Doom and myself present. He offered a vague wave toward the open bathroom door.

"All clean and purty now, Miz Canary," he mumbled, then moved toward the door to the corridor.

"Call me Linda, Daniel," the woman invited. That drew the suggestion of a smile from him, but he kept going, head down, closing the door behind him.

"Why are you here, Mr. Doom?" Linda Jensen wanted to know, suddenly curious. She had paused in her makeup removal efforts and was staring at us quizzically.

"I would say to protect you," Doom stated. "You know about the dead dog?"

"Only through the heartbroken mumblings of Bob Buchman." There was a twist of the lips with her statement that made her appear less attractive. "He wouldn't say whether he would be here today, so I had to fire him."

"The show must go on!" I tossed in for effect. They only thing I got was a nasty look from Doom. I don't know whether Linda Jensen was listening.

"There has to be a reason someone has been trying to kill you," Doom stated. "Do you have any idea who, or why?"

The songstress shook her head, while removing more cold cream. "Neither. Why am I a threat to anyone? Sure, I'm the divorced wife of a convicted killer, but I had nothing to do with anything illegal. I just sang in Jensen's nightclub until we were married."

"Well, there were some rather unusual paragraphs in the pre-nuptial agreement signed by yourself and Guns Jensen before your marriage," Doom reminded her.

The woman's face took on an exasperated expression. "Mr. Doom, understand something. I married Guns Jensen for what I might get out of it sooner or later. Guns understood that. On the other hand, he loved me then, and I know he loves me now. Leaving his wealth to me was his idea."

Doom nodded. "Ill-gotten or otherwise?"

She matched his nod, her tone taking on a note of harshness. "Ill-gotten or otherwise."

Doom seemed to be baiting the woman, which I didn't understand, but before he could continue, there was a knock at the door.

"Who is it?" Linda Jensen called. There was no reply, and the woman stood there, tense and scowling. She glanced at the two of us, then motioned to a screen in the corner. It was set up so an actress or actor could change clothes or costumes and continue a conversation while others were in the room.

Doom grabbed me by the arm and dragged me behind the screen, as there was another knock, this one heavier than before.

"Who is it?" Linda Jensen called, louder this time.

Chapter Twenty-two

Huddled behind the dressing screen with Doom, I looked over the top to see the door open toward me, blocking my view. I couldn't see who had entered, but I recognized the voice.

"Like I said, Linda, this last show is a real gem. It deserves celebration." It was Jack Sterling. From the sound of his voice, he seemed to be crossing the room. I felt a nudge in my ribs. Doom had a finger against the screen and was twisting it back and forth.

"I brought along a prize wine from my collection," Sterling was saying. "This is a Greek vintage, something I'm sure you'll like."

"I don't know whether I feel like celebrating right now," Linda Jensen told him.

"Just a glass or two and you'll feel fine," he urged.

"I know how much pressure you've been under. It hasn't been easy for any of us."

While they were talking, I dug the stock knife out of my pocket and opened the master blade, handing it to Doom. He nodded thanks and twisted the point of the knife back and forth against the screen's covering. In an instant, there was a hole that was probably an eighth inch in diameter.

"Why the seltzer water?" Linda wanted to know. "You don't mix it with the wine, do you?"

Sterling offered a chuckle, as Doom handed me back my knife, blade still open. "It pains me to say so, but my doctor has me off of booze of any kind. Nothing stronger than seltzer for now."

I began cutting my own peephole in the screen.

"Maybe I'll have some of your seltzer instead," the woman said. There was a troubled note in her tone.

"Then it wouldn't be a celebration," Sterling was saying as I put my eye to the hole. He had a corkscrew in hand and was pulling the cork from the bottle. A small tray with two tall wine glasses was on Linda's dressing table.

"Just a few sips, Linda," he wheedled. "You'll love it. The Greeks make a really fine wine."

I watched as Sterling tilted the bottle and almost filled one of the wine glasses. He handed it to her, then poured the open bottle of seltzer into the other glass, raising it in salute.

"To a great future with the show!" he toasted, tilting the glass of clear liquid to take a sip. All the time, though, his eyes were on Linda. She lifted the glass as though to take a sip, but frowned when it was near her lips.

"What's this odor?" she wanted to know. "I've never smelled anything like this before."

"This wine does have an unusual bouquet," Sterling declared, frowning. "Go ahead. You'll enjoy it, I promise."

That was when Doom stepped around the edge of the screen. "That's enough, Jack," he announced sternly. The studio owner whirled to face him.

"What're you doing in here?" Sterling demanded.

"Watching you try to poison the lady." Doom's tone was cold, and Linda stared at Sterling with what I would describe as fascinated horror. The wine glass fell from her hand.

"That's sheer nonsense," Sterling snarled. "What're you saying?" Meantime, I had come around the other side of the screen. He didn't seem surprised to see me.

"I've already said it," Doom stated. "If you weren't trying to poison her, *you* drink from that wine bottle!"

"My doctor won't let me," Sterling protested. "You heard what I told her."

"Your doctor isn't here," Doom told him. "Let me see you down a couple of good gulps."

With a sigh, Sterling turned to the tray still on the dressing table. He picked up the wine bottle by its neck, then, faster than I thought he could move, smashed it on the edge of the table, leaving the neck and jagged glass from the lower half in his hand. He grabbed Linda, jerking her toward him, while pressing the sharp glass against her throat.

"I'm taking her out of here," he said roughly, a wildness in his eyes I never expected to see.

"You just announced your guilt, Jack, but you made a mistake," Doom said quietly. "The curare in the wine would not kill her. Stomach acid would eat up the poison before it could get into her bloodstream."

Sterling looked surprised, glancing down at the dark wine from the bottle that marked the gray carpet. Then his narrowed eyes came back to Doom, who shook his head, taking a step toward him. I hoped Doom wasn't going to try to do anything heroic. That stuff's for television and fools. When a lady's life is in jeopardy, damage control becomes the chief issue.

Sterling pressed the edge of broken glass more firmly against the woman's neck. She wriggled, and a trace of blood began to course down the skin of her throat. Doom stopped in his tracks, though his tone remained conversational.

"You thought your experiment with the dog proved something. You were trying to force feed it curare with a hypodermic needle while giving him dog treats. Somehow the needle penetrated the back of the dog's throat and the curare went into his bloodstream—*that's* what killed Mark Anthony."

While Doom was talking, I walked over to the door, blocking it. Sterling, the jagged glass still pressed to the woman's throat, turned his attention to me.

"We're going out of here, Cougar. Don't try to stop us."

I didn't have to stop him. Behind him, the door to the bathroom swung open. Daniel Denny, no longer the shuffling senior citizen, began edging across the carpet. I couldn't see what he had hidden in his right hand, but in his left was what looked like a 9mm Beretta. It was leveled at Sterling's back.

"The smartest thing you could do is surrender," Doom declared. "There's a man behind you with a gun."

"Don't try that old gag on me, Doom!" Sterling snarled, starting to push the woman toward me. "Get out of the way, Cougar!"

My smile must have served as a warning. Sterling suddenly reacted, whirling around, but Denny was on him, using his gun barrel to hit the wrist holding the broken bottle. The broken bottle flew across the room and shattered against the wall. In the same instant, Daniel Denny plunged a hypodermic needle into Sterling's neck, using his other hand. I could see that the plastic container was half full of a brown liquid. But when Denny jerked it free of the pulsing flesh, the tube was empty. In the same instant, he pulled Linda from the man's grasp, whirling her across the room. Doom caught her to keep her from falling.

"Try that for size!" Denny snarled, as he stepped away from the surprised and frightened man. Sterling simply stood there, massaging the side of his neck, lips twisted in a show of outright horror.

I knew then why something about Denny had appeared out of kilter. The hair was white, the bushy eyebrows were white, but the stubbly beard was salt-and-pepper gray. It doesn't happen that way—the beard is always the first to turn white!

The needle had been plunged into Sterling's carotid artery, the one that carried blood to the brain. He staggered back, then fell to the floor. I don't know whether he had simply fainted or the poison had taken effect that fast. Denny stood over him, looking for any sign of life. Then he turned to look at us, hoisting the hypodermic kit for our inspection.

"Found it in his bathroom medicine cabinet. I guess what was left he couldn't get into the wine bottle." Then he tossed the tube and attached needle into the corner near Sterling's body. He did the same with the gun he had been holding.

"You can take off the wig now, Guns," I told him. He ignored me, turning to his ex-wife, who slipped into his arms, suddenly sobbing. I glanced toward the bathroom. It had two doors, I noted. It was shared by whomever had the adjoining dressing room. That was how Guns Jensen was able to come back.

Doom was staring at Guns and Linda Jensen, still reeling from the turn of events. I took it upon myself to cross the room and bend beside the body, checking for a pulse in the neck. There was none. I glanced at Doom and shook my head.

The door suddenly swung open beside me and Lieutenant Brock was standing there, a gun in his hand. He looked around the room, eyes shifting from one person to another.

"What's going on here?" he demanded. Then he nodded to the body on the floor. "Is he dead?"

"I hope so," Guns Jensen replied, reaching up to strip off the wig with the hand that wasn't holding Linda. Then he dropped the wig and pulled off the fake eyebrows one at a time.

"Guns!" Brock exploded. His hand tightened on his

handgun. Guns Jensen offered him a twisted, ironic grin, raising both hands to shoulder level.

"I'm th' one who called to invite you," he announced quietly. Over Linda's shoulder, he nodded to Sterling's still figure. "He was tryin' t'kill my wife. I took him out with his own poison." He looked down at Linda, still huddled against his shoulder, comforted apparently by the protective arm around her.

"I'm a little involved here, Lieutenant, but for all practical purposes, I'm surrendering to you. I'm unarmed."

At that point Linda drew back, eyes still tearful. She looked at Jensen's face. "I knew when you broke out it was to protect me," she said tearfully. "But this kills your appeal."

Guns held her then at arms length, offering a sad little smile. "The appeal was just a formality, honey. It's something the state of California has to do. They had me cold, and it was only a matter of time before they stick me in that little green room up there at the prison."

Brock had found a chair in the corner and was sitting on the edge of it, gun still leveled. Guns Jensen glanced at him, then nodded toward the corpse.

"Two for one ain't such a bad trade, Brock. They can't gas me more'n once, can they?"

Chapter Twenty-three

"Why didn't you cover him with your gun when you stepped around the screen?" I asked Doom later. He cast me one of his raised eyebrow glances, shaking his head.

"I didn't *have* a gun. Why didn't you?"

"I didn't have a gun, either." I couldn't hold back a chuckle. "I'm glad it's over. Everything turned out pretty well, except for Jack Sterling. And Guns Jensen." That brought a pensive look from Doom.

"I think Guns is as happy as possible under the circumstances. According to Linda, he'd accepted the fact that he's going to be executed. He just wishes they'd get it over with."

"How's she doing?" I wanted to know, remembering the way she had clung to Guns in her dressing room.

"I think she's feeling guilty that she's never really been able to love him. That could be especially true since he broke out of jail to protect her."

Jonathan Doom and I were seated in front of the window, watching traffic and sipping his Kona coffee. It had been three days since the showdown at the late Jack Sterling's studio. Doom had finally found his notes on curare and discovered the reason he had rejected the script years earlier. The script used curare used as an ingested poison in a murder plot. His own research had told him that unless it was a really massive dose, a person's stomach acid would destroy the poison before it could be effective. It had to be introduced directly into the bloodstream.

Now, these many years later, he told me he was sure Jack Sterling had submitted that old script to him under a pen name. He had returned it to the literary agent without explaining his own findings.

Further investigation revealed that Sterling was only days away from foreclosure on his business for an unpaid mortgage. In addition, the Federal Communications Commission was at the point of revoking the license for the TV station over bad programming, and the Internal Revenue Service was after him, as well.

He had told us Linda Jensen had paid money up front for production and had also bought a completion bond. That bond actually had been the million-dollar insurance policy. Sterling's corporation, it seemed, was the beneficiary of the policy. Under the terms of the written agreement, she could not dip into Guns' money until he was dead or his appeals had been exhausted, and she needed money to finance what she hoped would be a new career. Sterling wasn't offering much in the way of credit any more. He'd financed too many unsuccessful shows. When she made Sterling the beneficiary, Linda hadn't realized the insurance policy could be her own death sentence.

Doom had no objections when I told him I was feeding the whole story to Sam Light. In fact, he was happy with the story that appeared that same morning in the West Coast newspapers. As he put it, "Sam made Guns Jensen a bigger hero than either you or I, but at least he spelled my name right!"

Earlier, Doom had pointed out another Sam Light byline on the first page of the financial section. Light had interviewed Simon Teller in Rio by telephone. The multimillionaire had stated his wife and son had fallen in love with the city. As a result, he was switching headquarters for his international enterprises to Brazil from Los Angeles.

The article had included a number of reasons why the Tellers had decided on the move, none of them making any mention of adoptions, phony nurses, or badly kept secrets. It was all strictly business.

"Sam handled that well," Doom conceded. "Teller has asked me to get with his lawyers and see that the old cook is pensioned off. He wants Maria to be sent down to Rio. He's already talked to her about it. Then he wants the furniture sold. His office staff here will clean out his personal papers in his den."

"That leaves the stuff of the spurious Helen Boyd," I pointed out.

"I'll take care of that myself," Doom told me.

"Here. This wasn't of much help." I dug into my

jacket pocket for the address book I had put there some days before. "This and all of her personal papers such as the certificates and diplomas should go to her dad back in Iowa. I'm sure you can think of some reason why they're turning up now."

I paused to give him a thoughtful glance. "Sam Light knows why Toni Teller was so upset all those months."

"Do you know why?" Doom wanted to know. "And is he going to print anything on it?"

The answers to those questions were a respective yes and no.

"I have some suspicions, but I don't really know the actual reason," Doom admitted.

"Little Brian is Toni's own son." I repeated what Light had told me. "The boy was born out there in Covina at the home, then Toni put him up for adoption. Apparently, Helen Boyd was working there when all this went down. After Toni married Simon Teller, she didn't tell her new husband the child was hers, but talked him into adopting him."

Doom nodded his understanding. "She was afraid of what Teller would think if the truth came out and Boyd took full advantage. It could have been solved so easily, too, if Toni and Simon had just been honest with each other. Before their marriage, he paid for an investigation of her past. He knew about Brian's birth. He even knew the boy they decided to adopt was her son, but he didn't want to accuse her of being dishonest! That had to be the way of it."

"That's pretty much the way Light has it. He started following the paper trail on the adoption, Toni and the home. It all fit together in the end, but that was for his own amusement," I said. "He sees no reason to dig up all the dirt."

Doom pushed himself up from his seat, picking up his empty cup and reaching for mine. "More coffee?"

I shook my head, getting on my feet, too. "Nope. I just came by to tell you I'm quitting."

"Quitting?" Doom almost dropped the cup. I didn't expect him to understand, but he deserved some sort of explanation.

"It's hard to put into words, but all the time I've been working for you, I've had the feeling I've been getting involved in other people's lives to the point that I have no life of my own." I hesitated for a moment, while Doom stared at me, offering that familiar scowl. "It's like this is all a movie or a TV show. I'm an actor in it, but nobody's given me a copy of the script."

"But this isn't all that different from what you've been doing," Doom declared, not understanding at all.

I shook my head, matching his scowl. "When I fall a horse or dive off a cliff, I'm done with the stunt right then. I pick up my check and go back to being Charlie Cougar, Native American. I can be me." I shook my head, again, looking him in the eye. "That's the best I can explain it."

Doom offered a chuckle and returned to his seat, putting the cup back on the coffee table. He started to laugh hard, rocking back and forth in his chair, while I stood watching, not understanding his behavior. Finally, he looked up at me.

"You're not going to believe this, Charlie, but Linda

Jensen wants to finance a TV special. She wants to call it *The Return of Jonathan Doom*! Her whole idea is to tell the story of what we've just been through and make Guns look like a hero!"

"Well, that might do something for the guilt she's feeling, and it ought to work out great for you." I picked up my hat from a low table and tipped over one eye. "I think that's what I've just been talking about."

"But she wants *you* to play the role of Charlie Cougar," Doom declared, still laughing. I shook my head.

"Not a chance, but be sure she gets an Indian to do the role. There's a whole workshop of Native Americans right here in Hollywood. Most of them are fine actors," I told him. He was still laughing at something, maybe the irony, as I closed the door to his condo for the last time.

I'd have to call the Stuntmen's Association to see about work. But even that would have to wait until after Sue Talllfeather's spring break. And if I was going to meet her mother, my first act should be to get a haircut.

I was beginning to look like an actor!